Praise for *Riptide*

"Scheibe's story is rich with details, real-life problems, and characters you want to hang out with. You will feel its pull."

—Jennifer Ziegler, author of
How Not to Be Popular

Riptide

For Eric,
who took me surfing on our first date.

LINDSEY SCHEIBE

One summer.
Endless possibilities.

flux™
Woodbury, Minnesota

First Edition
First Printing, 2013

Book design by Bob Gaul
Cover design by Lisa Novak
Cover image: Woman © iStockphoto.com/Stígur Karlsson

Flux, an imprint of Llewellyn Worldwide Ltd.

This is a work of fiction. Names, characters, places, and incidents are either the product of the author's imagination or are used fictitiously, and any resemblance to actual persons living or dead, business establishments, events, or locales is entirely coincidental. Cover model used for illustrative purposes only and may not endorse or represent the book's subject.

Library of Congress Cataloging-in-Publication Data
Scheibe, Lindsey.
  Riptide/Lindsey Scheibe.—First edition.
      pages cm
  Summary: "While training for a surfing competition to earn a college scholarship, Grace Parker struggles with her feelings toward her best friend Ford Watson and tries to conceal her family's toxic dynamics"—Provided by the publisher.
  ISBN 978-0-7387-3594-8
[1. Surfing—Fiction. 2. Best friends—Fiction. 3. Friendship—Fiction. 4. Dating (Social customs)—Fiction. 5. Child abuse—Fiction. 6. San Diego (Calif.)—Fiction.] I. Title.
  PZ7.S3427Ri 2013
  [Fic]—dc23
                                                            2012048951

Flux
Llewellyn Worldwide Ltd.
2143 Wooddale Drive
Woodbury, MN 55125-2989
www.fluxnow.com

Printed in the United States of America

Surfer Lingo

| Comb |

A comb is used to scrape the wax on the
surfboard to create texture and friction.

| Duck Dive |

When a big wave is coming, a surfer can push
the surfboard underneath the water and let the wave
pull them below it, which is easier than getting
hammered by the top side of the wave.

| Foamies |

Foamies are leftover waves that crash in closer to shore;
they aren't as clean and have a lot more whitewater.
Most people learn to surf on foamies, since these waves
are less powerful and don't require much paddling to get
to. The consequences of falling are less severe also.

| Leash |

The leash goes around a surfer's ankle and keeps the board
from escaping if the surfer falls off the board. A surfboard
not connected to a surfer and propelled around freely by
the ocean can be dangerous. It would also require that
the surfer to return to shore to fetch the board, and then
paddle all the way back out to make a second attempt.

| Lineup |

Surfers waiting to catch their next ride sit in a loosely formed lineup where people "know" when it's their go. It's also the area where it's easiest to wait for and catch good waves. The lineup is not always based on who was there first. Sometimes seniority and/or localism comes into play.

| Party Waves |

Party waves are crowded waves where there are multiple surfers trying to catch/ride the same wave.

| Riptide |

A riptide is a strong current that pulls away from the shore. Riptides typically occur along sand breaks, where an underwater sandbar (or other topography) changes and forms a strong seaward current that can take objects and people out to sea. In order for someone to get out of a riptide, they need to paddle sideways to exit the current, or risk exhausting themselves as they panic to swim to shore only to go nowhere.

| Wax |

Wax is used to help surfers stick to their board, and also to wick the water off the board so the board is less slick.

one

Surfing is for life.
—Bruce Jenkins, *North Shore Chronicles*

I stretch out my legs, enjoying the hot sand against my calves. Early morning sun creates an orange sheen on the ocean as I search for a big set of waves. The endless white formations roll in; lines of blurred corduroy become distinct opportunities—or not—as they roll closer to the local surf break. A few surfers are already out there, dotting the horizon and catching waves. Alluring, sexy waves. The kind that promise to wash away anything but the moment you're riding them.

I look over my shoulder to see Ford walking toward me, his board under his arm. He's late. But no point in being frustrated. Ford is Ford. I put up with it because he's one of the major reasons I'm sane. Well, him and surfing. I flex my toes and bend them down, digging them into the sand. Ford's been my best friend since the summer before sophomore year—he was a newbie from Huntington, wearing surfer clothes and looking the part. I was obsessed with surfing that entire summer. After a couple of arguments about which surfers on the junior tour had the best sessions on YouTube videos, we agreed to disagree until one of us kicked enough ass to compete.

Ford lays his board down and sits next to me. "There's a set coming in and you're catching rays? C'mon on now, Grace."

"At least I show up early to pay homage to the waves. Where's your dedication, Mr. Surf God?"

"I'm dedicated to my friends and the waves. It's Esmerelda's fault I'm late."

Ford could drive almost any truck in existence, as tricked-out as it gets. But he prefers Esmerelda, a wonderful old beater he can work on. He probably had to coax her to life this morning. Lately, she's had a funny knocking sound.

I try not to check him out too obviously. His dark legs and lean body have changed for the better since last summer. I can't help crushing on him, but we're BFs and that's off-limits. Besides, every ounce of energy I have this summer is going toward figuring out how to get a surf scholarship to UCSD.

He kicks off his Reefs and I add, "Nice board shorts. You have excellent taste."

"Yeah, since you picked them out, Gidget." His eyebrows rise and his left dimple shows. There's a playful challenge in his grin, one I can't ignore.

"Oh yeah? Gidget?" When people hear that name, regular folks might not know what it means. Older folks might think about the old movies, TV series, or books. But when surfers hear "Gidget," they usually think about a woman who still gets listed as one of the top surfer girls ever. They also think "pint-sized."

Standing up to my full height, I come eye-to-chest with Ford. I give him my best intimidating stare. Fighting a smile probably isn't helping the stare-down thing.

Ford throws his head back and laughs. I step toward him, hands on my hips. In one quick swoop, he bends down and slings me over his shoulder. I hang onto his torso, trying to lessen the jostle, as he runs toward the water.

Flailing and slapping his back, I protest. "Ford Watson, put me down."

"Ford *Watson*," he mocks, simultaneously laughing and wading into knee-deep water before tossing me in. I squeal in protest at the cold. My butt hits the hard sand before I spring up, ready to get even, but by the time I wipe salty water from my eyes Ford is on the beach waxing his board—a ten-foot Stewart Regal, single fin. The seductiveness of his surfboard is ridiculous, a new take on a retro design. Tribal spears hug the outsides of the board, which is a blue that blends in with the ocean, making him a god commanding the waves.

Charging out of the water, I make a beeline for him.

He waves me off. "Aww. Be a good sport. Go wax your board."

"Fine, but only 'cause a solid set is coming in."

Since it's the summer before senior year, this is *the* year—my last chance to get noticed by college surf coaches. If I want to have a snowball's chance in the Bahamas of making it happen, then I gotta tweak my skills and make a local presence. That's what it takes to get noticed.

My board is an old yellow beak-nosed from the 70s. It's a six-foot ten-inch Bing model with faded red lettering. Dings show off the vintage factor, if the shape of the nose weren't telltale enough. Thin red lines outline the edges. A couple of patches draw attention, screaming *fixed by girl owner*. I love it.

"Grace, the waves ain't gonna wait."

I flick sand at Ford's feet. Feeling antsy to catch some, I go tug on my summer wetsuit. It may be June, but the water around here is still in the upper sixties.

I slide my suit over my legs and hop a little as I try to pull it over my shoulders. My boobs jiggle a little in the process. I glance over at Ford and notice how he turns his head quickly. I tug at the sleeves of my wetsuit, slightly amused and slightly embarrassed. I turn around so he can zip me up. It's not like I can't; it's just something nice he does for me.

My leash is all knotted up. Ford untangles it and attaches it to my surfboard. Most boards have a place embedded on the underbelly to attach the leash, but for some reason, mine is special. It attaches to the fin.

"Thanks, Ford."

"I'll be an old man by the time you're finished if I don't help."

"Whatev."

I wax my board while he grabs my ankle, attaching my leash. For a split second his hand lingers there. Last night's dream flickers and I stand up, aware of the inch of skin his hand touched. I grab my board and run toward the water with a long-short, long-short gallop as my leash holds one leg back.

"Last one in loads the boards," I holler, running at half speed and knowing there's no chance of Ford catching me when I'm this far ahead.

I reach the waterline, toss my board in victoriously, wade out as far as I can, and then begin the arduous task of getting raked over as I paddle out.

Ford may have reached the water second, but he paddles fast and soon makes it out there to the big dogs waiting for the Wave.

I keep my eye on the locals as I paddle out to the lineup. The water turns rough as a set of waves pass through. I sputter, hang on, and try to paddle past. Two strokes forward, one knocked back. After repeating this scenario several times, I join the rest of the surfers.

"Hey, Parker. Over here," Ford directs, staking his claim on me. Really, he's protecting me from a few hormone-raging, I-only-think-below-the-waist potheads. Though not all surf guys are like that. There really are a lot of super-talented, artsy surfers... contrary to some people's opinions, like my mom's...

The two other girls out here, Carrie and Talia, usually

hang together. They're stud surfers and sometimes I wish we could be friends. But my mom taught me a long time ago that women aren't to be trusted. Most girls would think I'm a weirdo or something anyway, because I wouldn't have a lot to say. The great thing about having guy friends is not having to talk about things you don't want to.

I paddle to Ford. He's straddling his longboard, black hair glistening; he greets me with a grin. His left dimple makes me think of the practical jokes he pulled on me after we first met. It also draws my eyes to his full lips.

When I reach his vicinity, I push up off my board and straddle it. Our boards bob up and down, announcing the next set's arrival.

Damien, a local surfer with gorgeous dreads, says, "Hey babe. Why don't you come catch some waves over here? They're a lot bigger." His insinuation is obvious, but I kind of enjoy being noticed even if he has a reputation for being a horndog. Personally, I think his reputation is more smoke than fire.

Ford steps in. "Prove it."

The other guys laugh. A few make the *ooh whatcha gonna do now* sound.

Even though Damien talks big, I think he's really a good guy. He's always been nice to me. I don't understand that instant rivalry Ford feels toward Damien.

The perfect wave comes our way. It's solid, peeling off the water into a tight curl while the face of it keeps growing. Ford starts paddling to snag it at the crucial moment.

I laugh; he's freaking awesome. He comes down off the face, does a bottom turn, and carves down the line to the right. He turns up and down the face the rest of the ride before he exits the wave and paddles toward me.

"Gnar ride, man," I say.

Ford basks in the warmth of my praise like a Beach Betty soaking up sun. With a *beat that* smirk, he looks toward Damien and shoots him the bird using both hands.

Damien happily returns the greeting and I try not to laugh. Damien's so cute about giving the one-fingered salute.

Ford says, "Hey, this next one's yours."

I look over my shoulder to see an epic wave barreling toward us.

"Hello? Look at the size of that monster."

"Parker. It's *your* turn." Ford always pushes me. "C'mon. Represent the ladies."

Ford knows what to say to get my dander up. I eye the wave and paddle for dear life. If I don't catch it, I'll drown trying. The wave catches up to me, and I start to get sucked up to the top. Falling off your board is one thing, but getting stuck in the wave when it comes crashing down is another. The force of the water pummels you, and rolls you until you don't know which end is up. Desperate, I try to paddle my way back toward the bottom of the wave. To represent. To show the guys what's up. More than anything, to prove to myself I'm tough.

I pop up on deck, right foot forward. I barely make the bottom turn, and then I notice the wave curling over my shoulders. For the first time in my life, I'm inside the barrel of a wave. Amped, I let out a tribal yell. The rush is incredible. Zooming through a wall of water, still breathing like normal, I enjoy the magic of feeling free and alone. I would stay in this water wonderland forever if I could. But the ride won't last; I bear down and transfer my weight to my front foot, accelerating my speed, and throw my left arm out to graze the wall of water as I shoot through it before it crumbles.

Euphoric, I cut back and ride what's left of the line. Cheers erupt. Whistles and applause. I paddle back toward the group. I swear I'm on top of the freaking world. Ford winks and gives me the *sweet move* thumbs-up. The two of us might be acting low-key, but the truth is, I've trained for this moment. Hard work makes victory that much sweeter. The whooshing sound of being barreled, and the feeling of running my hand through an ocean wall, play on repeat as I make my way toward the crew.

After another hour of surfing—and laughing at the guys jawing back and forth about their boards, their "packages," and the waves—I paddle in. Actually, I catch a wave and ride it in as long as I can, savoring the floating, lazy sensation of letting the ocean carry me toward shore until I'm in knee-deep water.

Once my feet hit the sand, I walk out of my Pacific haven and disengage my leash. That's when I feel the reality of life hit me head-on. I dig frantically through my bag and slather on more sunscreen in case the ocean washed off the first application. Then I fish for my visor and sunglasses. If I come home with one more sunburn I'm gonna be grounded for life, or worse—I'll receive the hour-long lecture about skin cancer, leathery skin, and rapid aging.

It's fun watching the breakers roll in and surfers catching rides. There are some girls who are ripping extra hard this morning. It's hypnotic watching them. Women bring fluidity and grace to the sport that not many men can claim. Watching a woman catch a wave is like watching a dance where the partners take turns leading.

Doubt creeps in like the ocean tide. My getting barreled once, here at Ponto, won't attract buzz. There are so many more tricks to learn, and I'm not even sure I can repeat today's victory. How much was luck and how much was preparation? Then I remember a quote Ford once wrote on a notecard for me to carry in my wallet, since he knows what a freak I am about quotes.

> *Luck is what happens when preparation meets opportunity.*—Lucius Annaeus Seneca

I plop down in the sand and frown, wondering how in the world I'm going to convince my mom to let me enter a couple of local comps in the fall, not to mention wanting to go to college in-state. Maybe I can get Dad to help convince her on the competition front, but that will be about as tricky as catching a seven-foot double-up at Big Rock. I grab my surfboard wax and play around with it, molding it with my fingers.

For me, surfing is survival. It transcends everyday life; it's all about the ride and the moment.

Every.

Single.

Time.

Everything else disappears.

two

mija: *contraction of "mi" and "hija" ("my" and "daughter"), used as a term of endearment*

I set my board down on the sand and nudge Grace's foot with mine, so freaking proud of her. "So about that tube ride…"

She knocks her hoodie back and does a seated victory dance, complete with squeal, while bouncing her feet in the sand.

I sit down by her, enjoying how cute she is when she gets excited. "Chill. Don't let it go to your head or I'm gonna have to buy you a visor three times bigger."

"Whatever. You know you're proud of me." She pokes my chest.

"You know, I charge people for that." I brush wet hair out of my face.

She laughs at my dumb joke. "Really? I thought it was the other way around."

"Ha ha. And while we're on our little bragfest, I got news." Holding this in, waiting for the perfect moment to share, has been epic hard.

She crinkles her nose. "What kind?"

"News of the one-more-reason-moms-in-San-Diego-County-would-love-for-me-to-date-their-daughter variety." I'm half joking about that. Her mom always seems so stiff; it feels like she's icing me out.

Grace rolls her eyes. "Well?"

"I've got an internship."

"Where?"

I bust out with a massive smile. "At the best law firm in town."

She scrunches her brows together. "Haha. Funny. You losing surf time over the summer, on purpose? I haven't heard Dad say anything about that. Besides, you would've asked me to hook you up, right? I mean, I do have the connections."

Her response floors me. "Really? You don't think I could get an internship on my own?"

"C'mon," Grace says. "That's not how I meant it. It's just that if you really were going for an internship at my dad's firm, I would think you'd have told me. And I think my dad would've said something about giving you a spot on his how-I'm-going-to-make-senior-partner program. That's all."

"Well, one, I did go for it, and two, remember that my first name isn't technically Ford—it's Ferdinand. If your dad had interviewed me, he would have found out just who this 'Ferdinand Watson' was. It's not like Watson is a unique last name! C'mon, I wanted to be treated like anybody else. No favors. But apparently he was caught up in some major case, so some junior-partner person met with me. And, by the way, three—your dad is like a freaking hero. His last high-profile pro bono case, where he saved that little old lady from deportation? He kicked some major ass. This internship is huge, and I thought you'd be ecstatic for me. Guess I was confused."

Grace lunges toward me and gives me a big hug. "Hey, I'm sorry."

I wrap my arms around her, my forearms resting across the top of her hips, fingers curved around her waist. She leans into me and rests against me, like for this minute everything unspoken that weighs down on her is in my hands. I wish I knew what goes on in Grace's head when she stares off, looking lost.

She pulls back and her smile is sweet as honey. "Congrats. Really. It'll be huge for your college apps, and I think you'll be awesome. They're lucky to have you. And you're right, Dad kicks major ass."

I pull her back for a quick hug and nuzzle the top of her head with my chin, wishing this hug was something more than it is. "Thanks, Grace."

"I really am—happy—for you. Let's celebrate."

I pull back and grin. "With a date?"

Crap.

Grace has this panicked look. She grabs her bag and digs

13

around. She plucks her ChapStick, opens it, and smears it nervously across her lips. "Um. Sure, we can totally go on a friend date."

Crash and burn. I should have been smoother. Been romantic.

Retreat, retreat.

I frown. "Okay. Well, I'm pretty booked this week getting ready for the internship. How about we just do lunch like normal?"

Grace grins, and the awkwardness of the moment passes. "Let's grab a bite to eat. I'm starving."

"Translation: Why don't we go to Ford's house, where he'll fix me tortillas with chorizo and eggs?"

"Well?"

"Fine," I say. "I'll fix you lunch, but only 'cause my cooking blows yours away."

Grace wags her finger at me, all cute. "I *know* you didn't go there. I know you didn't. A few burnt pieces of toast and a gal's reputation goes down the tubes. Because I'm a nice girl and all, I'm gonna pretend you didn't say that."

———

Some bunnies are just that—bunnies who like to get all fancy but got nothing to say. They're blank boards, nothing on them. And, for sure, there are plenty of hotties out there. But Grace? She's off the charts—every guy with a brain and a pair of nads drools when she walks past in those comfy surf T-shirts that hug her in all the right ways.

To me, she's hot. She's fun. She surfs, likes to work out. Laughs at my dumb jokes. She's cool. When I pull up to the beach, Grace sitting next to me in Esmerelda, I know all the guys are wishing she was in their truck instead, letting them help her with her surfboard.

For the past two years, I haven't progressed one bit past the best-friend-o-meter. And I've been so gone over Grace that I haven't even considered another girl. Heck, I talk big in the lineup, but what guy doesn't? The truth is, I'm inexperienced when it comes to girls. Grace is the only one I've had eyes for and she hasn't shown interest, at least not that I can be sure about. This summer it's time to steer my own ship, and there are two destinations I plan on sailing for: one, dating Grace, and two, impressing colleges with my internship at one of the top law firms in San Diego. So far, number one ain't looking so hot. 'Cause the whole deer-in-the-headlights *sure, we can go on a friend date*? Not exactly encouraging.

The ride to my house is filled with music, no convo, and mental replays of this morning. I wish Grace had been more excited about my internship. Sometimes I feel like she's hot and cold about things. About me. Sometimes chasing her gets me all bent, like a crap end to a decent ride.

I pull up the gravel drive to *mi casa*, listening to the usual crunch of pebbles under my wheels. Esmerelda's engine cuts with a sigh and I hop out. As I walk around the front of the car, Grace bursts out of the truck, legs flailing cartoon-style as she lands on the grass.

She mutters, "Stupid door sticks."

I crack up.

She whacks me on the arm. "You *know*—it's easier to open the door from the outside."

"If someone would wait, instead of getting her panties in a wad, I might be able to get to the door in time to help out."

"If someone didn't feel the need to drive around in an old truck with rusted hinges … " Her voice fades off in a singsong trail.

"Sacrilege! Wash that mouth out with soap."

She smiles and shakes her head.

"Careful now, Esmerelda's sensitive."

Grace follows me up the gravel path and then separates when I start crossing the grass. She keeps to the sidewalk like always. For a while, I told her it's okay to walk on our grass. Grass is grass. You know? But Grace can't help herself. It's like she's destined to color inside the lines. Me? I figure lines are more of a suggestion—like speed limits.

All the windows are open and the screen door is letting the breeze into the house, which means one thing. Ma, God help us all, is on a cleaning spree. Unfortunately, she's not really good at it. So, there will be piles of laundry left on the couch or a cleaning rag abandoned on the countertop, mid-swipe. Anytime I've seen the inside of Grace's house, it's spotless. It's dumb, but sometimes I'm kind of embarrassed about the little messes here and there.

We walk through the entry and I hurry past what Grace calls *The Great Wall of Watsons*. Basically, it's the worst wall in America. It's chock-full of crap like little league plaques, karate trophies, and Ma's four diplomas. Yep, that's four. Most people are content to get a bachelor's. Some spring for a master's and a few driven souls get their doctorates. But Ma? She had to get two master's degrees. It drives me nuts how Grace lingers when we pass the way-to-go show. She knows it too.

"*Mammi*. Grace and I are home for lunch."

Ma enters from the hallway.

Grace says, "Great skirt, Mrs. Watson."

Ma pads across, gives me a big hug, and plants a loud kiss on my cheek. Then she wipes at my hair like I'm in kindergarten. "*Mammi*! Come on." I bob away from her like a boxer, footwork included. This is the routine. Never fails. I look over at Grace, slightly embarrassed again.

Her response? A tiny amused smirk.

I look back at Ma and roll my eyes, which is quickly returned with a swat to the top of my head, "Ah *Mammi*…"

"Well, don't roll your eyes at me."

"I wasn't—" Crap. The Look. That one. I back off fast. "Okay okay, I was just kidding. Sorry."

Grace laughs hysterically.

"Ah, *mijo*." Ma waves at me as if I have no right to embarrassment. She greets Grace. "*Mija*." Ma chuckles and gives her a big hug and smooch on the cheek. She pulls back and looks her up and down, wagging her long red nail, which I assume means she thinks Grace needs to fatten up. She usually makes some sort of reference to anyone's need to eat more.

"Grace, it's good to see you. You're so tan—I might be

able to get away with claiming you as my own. *Mijo*, fix this girl some lunch."

Which, of course, is the whole reason we're here.

Ma asks, "Weren't you two out surfing?"

"Yes, and we're starving," Grace quickly responds.

Ma quips, "Which is the precise reason you need to get some real food in this girl. Now that the house is clean, I have research projects to grade." She wanders off down the hall humming, clueless about the mop still leaning against the kitchen counter. She's the stereotypical genius who can never find her laptop. And Dad? He almost always has grease stains rubbed into creases on his hands.

Ma is a marine biology professor at the University of San Diego, a guru in the field. Guru meaning badass, in all respects. She knows her stuff.

We *vámonos* to the kitchen. An article boasting the latest buzz on her most recent academic feat hangs on the refrigerator. It's titled *Patricia Watson—Local Genius*. I slide the article down and say, "There goes Mom, kicking butt and taking names."

"Must run in the family."

"Me? Ha." I open the fridge and hum while sorting through the ridiculously crowded shelves. Fixing vehicles and excelling in academics runs in our family; cleaning out the refrigerator does not. In fact, I'd go so far as to say it's a dirty phrase in our house.

I grab a carton of eggs, *queso fresco,* chorizo, and then the key to it all, a container full of Ma's homemade tortillas.

Grace says, "Maybe this will fatten me up."

"*Ai.*" I focus my energy on chopping the chorizo before I say, "You don't need to be fattened up, and you don't need to lose weight."

"Says you. My curves barely exist." Grace sidles over and bumps her hip against me as if to prove her point. The girl has some curves. Enough curves to make my heart beat faster.

"Don't underestimate yourself." She lets loose a small smile. Score.

I love cooking, and if it weren't for the fact that I want to actually do something with my life like help people, especially my peeps, I might go all gourmet chef. I crack the eggs one-handed over the cast iron skillet. I let the eggshells rest in the palm of my hand and bump my hand from underneath to make the eggshells fly onto a nearby plate. I glance over at Grace to see if she was watching. Her smile widens. Bingo.

I focus on flipping the tortillas on the second skillet and try to come up with something to say. "So today was a great day, huh?"

"Yeah. It was."

Grace puts the magazine down and pours a cup of coffee, watching me flip the tortillas using my fingertips. Little bubbles of brown pop up on one. I add it to my *abuelita's* hand-stitched tortilla warmer, which she gave Ma when my folks married.

Even though we still aren't a couple, lunch this afternoon is different—and in a weird way. I think it might be different-good, but if that's true, then why'd she pull the friend card earlier?

I always have fun with Grace, but there's something about her lately; I can't quite put my finger on it. I've been making little comments here and there, like a litmus test for our relationship moving to the next level. Problem is, it feels like the results keep changing.

three

*Fairy tales do not tell children that
dragons exist. Children already know
that dragons exist. Fairy tales tell the
children that dragons can be killed.*
—G. K. Chesterton

During the ride back to my house, I try to hang on to the fun
from surfing this morning. But it's like it's not in my DNA.
That whole out-of-sight-out-of-mind thing only works when
I'm on my surfboard. When the ocean isn't there to com-
mand my attention or Ford isn't around making me laugh, I
get sucked back toward my family like it's a black hole. I've
spent my whole life keeping my worlds separate—school,
beach friends, home. And now, what with Ford interning for
my dad, two of them are colliding like particles in an atom
smasher. It's all I can do not to come unhinged.

I shake the thoughts out of my head and refocus on
the scenery as Ford slows Esmerelda to a stop. Dad's car

is parked in the drive. A sudden tightness in my stomach makes me clutch the edge of the seat.

Great, just great.

Ford says, "Smell ya later."

"Yeah, sure."

Ford uses his underarm to make a fart noise, indicating my lack of comeback, before Esmerelda burps a loud good-bye.

I carry my board over to the garage and lay it against the inside wall by the door. Then I plaster a smile on my face, steel my nerves, and walk inside the house via our immaculate laundry room.

It's best to get it over with and say hi to Dad. That's the only way to gauge his mood. I head over to the kitchen and then go into the living room.

He's combing through the mail, a mug of beer on the coffee table.

"Hey, Daddy. How's your morning been?"

"Could have been better. I came home to take a quick break and regroup. This Thompson case is getting out of control." He looks up and frowns. "Where have you been all day?"

"I went surfing with Ford, remember?" I shift my weight from side to side.

Dad flings an envelope on the coffee table, creating a trash pile that will be cleaned immediately after the mail has been sorted. "Are you sunburned? You know how your mother feels about too much sun. Let me see your arms." He grabs my arm to inspect it.

My eyes widen as I check out my skin with him. "No, I'm not sunburned, Daddy. I slathered sunscreen on this morning. The strongest stuff we have."

He drops my arm. He seems disappointed. "Have you done your chores?"

His hands are now full of mail; I relax a little. "No, I'll finish those this evening. I haven't had a chance to do them yet."

He tosses the papers down. His voice turns ugly. "You had time to surf."

"I'll start my chores now." I bite my lip.

He zeroes in on my fear like a shark sensing blood in the water. "What about your college applications?"

"Well, I'll do those after my chores."

"Well, which is it?" he growls. "Are you going to do your applications or your chores?"

"Both. Which would you like me to do first? Obviously, I'm not getting what you want me to do."

As soon as this flies out of my mouth, I know I've given him the opening he wants. Every muscle in my body tenses expectantly. I'm caught inside a twenty-foot swell and don't know a maneuver worth a damn.

His face turns red and it twists into something frightening and malicious. "Why, you little—" He raises his hand to hit me and pulls back just before making contact.

I flinch and cringe. God, I hate showing fear.

Instead of following through with it, he closes in on me and crushes my upper arm. "I don't care how you do it. You better get your damn work done by tonight. And I mean all of it."

I run down the hall before he decides to follow after me. Once I'm safe in my room, I slide down against the doorframe and cry without sound. As I hug my knees, I notice the red fingerprints on my arm. I touch them lightly, close my eyes, and lower my head between my knees. My existence diminishes like a boat on the horizon. I become nothing.

When it feels like everything is slipping out of my reach, I do what I always do. While hugging my favorite stuffed animal—a pajama-clad bear from when I was little—I open my journal of quotes and flip to a good one:

> *A woman is like a tea bag; you never know how strong she is until she gets into hot water.*—Eleanor Roosevelt

Quotes are buoys in the ocean. I hang on to them for sanity, for life, for hope. Quotes keep me going. Sometimes having someone else's words encourages me. They give shape to my feelings.

I should have lied. Told him I'd finished a stupid college app. Next time, I will. You'd think I'd have learned better by now, about lying to make things right. Whatever … what difference does it make?

I snap to it. There are applications to work on and chores to finish. I take a quick shower—the shower is one of the only places in my house where I feel safe—and let the hot water beat against my skin. Little drops constantly raining down, washing the finger marks off my arm. Washing the humiliation down the drain. Me wishing I could slip down those pipes and come out somewhere else. Anywhere else.

I wish I could stay in the shower forever, but I can't, so I shut it off. I'm determined to beat him at his own game. I'll accomplish everything with time to spare. So I throw some clothes on and get started. I vacuum the house and then sweep and mop the kitchen and bathrooms. I chip away at the tasks before me, taking mini-breaks to fill in tedious, never-ending blanks on college apps to places I don't want to attend.

By the time my mom arrives home from shopping, dusting the living room is the one thing unfinished. My dad hasn't spoken to me since earlier. He's engrossed in whatever case information he's reviewing. Whenever he has a particularly tough case, sometimes he works from home so no one from the office interrupts him. It's good for him but not for me.

Mom breezes in, shopping bags in hand. "Hey, kiddos. How was your afternoon?"

Dad answers, "Everything's great. I'm working on the Thompson case and Grace has been cleaning."

I quietly dust a lamp. He's so full of BS. It's an unwritten rule that we keep our mouth shut about Dad's "outbursts," and if it ever does come up, I get the whole *it's better to have a father than not* speech. Or *sure, you can call CPS and go live with someone else. Good luck on your foster family. Have you heard the horror stories from those kids?* And I know she's right. I've heard enough to know the grass isn't always greener.

"What's going on?" Mom asks, brows furrowed.

I shrug and say nothing. Maybe I'll say something next time we jog together. Then again, maybe not. She never cares enough to leave him. She never sees the shit go down either, which is real convenient. And it's not like the marks stay—or if they do, they aren't in the shape of hand. It could have been from falling on my surfboard. Right?

Mom surveys me. Her eyes move straight to the cutoff jean shorts I changed into. "I hope you're not planning on wearing those things out in public."

"No ma'am. I don't have any plans to go anywhere." Someday, I'm going to walk out of this house in whatever I want. Until then, frayed or unacceptable clothes get hidden in whatever bag I'm carrying when I walk out the door.

"They make it look like your parents can't afford to buy you anything better."

"I didn't want to risk getting bleach on my nice shorts."

She takes off her three-inch business heels and rubs at a frown line on her forehead. "Throw those out and go put on acceptable shorts for the dinner table—something tailored."

If I weren't in front of Miss Highbrow Fashion, aka Mom, I would so fake-barf at the mention of wearing something tailored. Bleh and grr.

"Jeez, Elaine. Frayed clothes are in right now. Grace always looks pretty."

Mom's lips are pursed in disapproval, but they're also closed and for that I'm thankful.

Dad changes the subject. "So, how was shopping? Show me all your goodies."

I glance over at Dad. We make eye contact. His face is kinder, almost sorry. The tension begins to fade away like it never happened.

I escape to my room. I hear Mom rattling on about the different purchases she made.

I close my eyes, exhausted.

———————

The alarm on my cell goes off. I slam my book shut, shoot off the couch, and make a running grab for my purse as I blast through the front door, relieved to see that I've beat my dad. I sit on the front porch steps and wait. After yesterday's showdown, a pleasant afternoon is what we need, if for nothing else than to clear the air between us. It makes Dad happy to spoil me. He likes to take me shopping and, before Ford got a truck, he would take me to the beach on Saturday mornings. Dad's the one who taught me how to surf and helped me learn how to know which wave would be a good ride.

He's the one who was with me when I bought my surfboard. Dad was driving me to the beach in his Jeep, his longish blond hair blowing all over the place. When I saw it in the window of Goodwill, I knew it was mine. "Dad, stop. Please! There's a surfboard for sale!"

Dad U-turned. It was one of those blue-sky days in our relationship. "Grace, are you sure you want a beat-up old board? I'd be happy to buy you a brand-new one with all the bells and whistles."

"No way. Old-school boards are cool. They have *history*."

Dad laughed and shrugged his shoulders. I like it when he laughs; it's contagious. Sometimes for a brief moment, I'm able to forget…

Mom had a conniption; she didn't like me surfing from day one. She never approved of anything that could be construed as dangerous. Somehow, surfing made it into that category. Maybe it's the sharks.

It's kind of ironic considering the state of our family dynamics.

I struggle with the mixed backwash of feelings about hanging out with Dad, about shopping with him. It's stressful at home, but outings with him are fun. It feels good and I know he cares. I mean, really… how many dads spend time with their kids? My grandfather didn't. He split before Dad ever entered the world, so Dad never met him. My grandfather wasn't around to protect Dad or teach him how to fight for himself when the neighborhood kids went after him, and *believe me, we didn't live in the kind of place you walk around in at night*.

I know shopping trips are his way of saying *sorry, I screwed up, and this is my apology*. But sometimes I wish he would just *say* it. But then I think about how hard his life was as a kid and how he's always been there for us. For my birthdays and Christmas. To take me surfing and shopping. Those are the times with my dad when I know I'm one hundred percent safe; when I know to savor what we have while we have it. And that's what I try to do.

Dad pulls up in his red convertible BMW, top down, a smile on his face. He reaches across and pushes open the door.

I hop in. "Thanks, Dad. You rock." Part of me means it; part of me knows I need to say it.

"Summer's just getting started and there are bound to be some special summer occasions. I can't have my daughter feeling anything less than a princess, now can I?" He pats my arm, backs out of our driveway, and speeds down the road.

As we shoot down the highway, a sense of cautious ease overtakes me. Nothing spoils a shopping day with Dad. These are moments he lives for. Moments he can be the good guy, the guy I know he wants to be all the time. I stay quiet, not wanting to mess things up, not wanting to make him frustrated. I can drive myself crazy with what ifs, or I can accept the reality of the moment. And this one should be good. The salty wind on my face tastes like freedom as we drive down the main drag to my favorite surf shop.

Dad pulls into the almost-empty parking lot. I exit his convertible and follow him toward Surf Stuff. A bell jingles when he opens a door that's covered in surf stickers. Loud music greets us, and a sick video of big wave surfing plays on a large flat-screen hanging on the back wall.

There's a sale rack I head straight for, eager to scope out the goods. Almost all the spring stuff is on sale. I grab three dresses that look pretty cute.

"Pick whatever you want." Dad reassures me with a smile.

"Thanks." I smile back and duck into a changing room.

I hang them up where I can compare them. An orange retro shift, a yellow empire-waist tank dress, and a classic white A-frame. According to Dad, all dresses should be mid-thigh to knee length. Not too short, not too long.

The shift is way too baggy and unflattering. My chest becomes non-existent. The A-frame is cute, but I have no bra that would be inconspicuous underneath. By the time I try on the empire waist, I'm feeling low on luck. I pull it over my head, adjust the straps, and voila. I feel confident and pretty.

I step outside to welcome Dad's opinion. He nods his approval.

"That looks good, honey. Do you have a lightweight sweater to wear with it?"

"Yep. Do you remember the short-sleeved white one from last summer?"

He smiles wide—it was a sweater he bought for me on a shopping trip. "Sure do. We bought it at Nordstrom's."

I grin and try not to remember the reason we bought it. "It's a perfect match."

"Good choice. Did you like the other dresses?" He glances at his watch.

I shrug. "They were cuter on the hangers."

I twirl around in front of the mirror. Dresses with the perfect twirl make me smile. This one swirls just right.

Dad tilts his head and smiles at me. "I can't believe my little girl's going off to college soon."

"Me neither." In this kind of situation, I play along, knowing he means every word, and I hang on them wishing this was our norm. It's hard not knowing what sets him off, living life trying to guess what color he wants me to fill in on his paint-by-numbers-with-no-color-key kit.

"And I think you've got a real shot at the Ivy Leagues if you don't mess up." Dad leans against the wall. "Was there anything else you want to browse?"

"Nope. This is perfect." I shift back and forth on my feet, feeling awkward but better. I know there's something really screwed up about this, and I feel like it's my fault somehow.

The only other dark cloud hanging over me is the fact that I'm not sure how to tell my parents I don't even want to leave San Diego for college—I want to attend UCSD.

four

internship: *fancy euphemism*
for copy grommet

It's the first day of my internship with Bristol and Wentworth, LLP, and I'm stuck in the world's worst traffic on Highway 1, sweating the fact that if things don't clear up, I'm going to be late. Not a stellar way to impress the boss who can make or break my college apps with his letter of recommendation.

Maybe it's lame to be excited about an internship—especially one that will cut out three mornings of surfing every week for the next eight weeks—but this is for all the Jorges out there. Last summer, one of my surfer buds, Jorge, disappeared. I didn't run into him for a few weeks at the beach and couldn't reach him on his cell. He never showed up at the skate park. This feeling in my gut that something was horribly wrong got confirmed when I ran into his neighbor, who told me Jorge and his mom had been deported. And then, a couple months later, things turned worse. Someday, I'm going to kick some INS courtroom ass.

I've never talked to Grace about how much this devastated me. It's too raw. Makes me feel exposed.

Ai. I see the exit, but traffic's moving at the pace of a snail taking a dump. It seems like forever before I pull into the parking garage for the Wentworth building.

By the time I open the fancy door to the office, not only am I late but I also have nasty sweat stains on the nerdy button-down Ma bought for my internship.

The admin reels back with an unapologetic look of disgust. Then she looks down at a piece of paper and says in a snooty tone, "Ferdinand. You're eleven minutes late, and you might want to reconsider your antiperspirant. I'm Teresa. Mr. Parker can't stand tardiness." Then she makes air quotes. "To be early is to be on time. To be on time is to be late. And to be late is unforgivable. Now head down the hall and hope he's not there waiting. Conference room G."

I hate it when people talk at me like that.

I stand there, thinking that I pictured this way different. Where's my funny comeback?

She waves me off quickly. "What are you doing? Run!"

I nod. "Uh, yeah. Thanks."

Then I walk-run down the hall, dodging suits, and say a quick prayer as I burst into the conference room. There's a lanky Asian-looking dude and a strikingly beautiful African-American girl sitting at a long table.

Of course, there's the backside of Mr. Parker's head

too. "You're late," he says as he swivels his chair around. When he sees me, he freezes for an instant.

"What's going on, Ford?"

Maybe not letting him know it was me applying was a bad idea. "Um ... I'm Ferdinand?"

An odd grin overcomes his previous expression of surprise. "Hmmm. Ford is short for Ferdinand? Well, I guess I would have already known how fortunate we are if I'd been at the interviews. I had more pressing things going on this year, like winning the Ricardo case. You're going to miss all those awesome summer waves?"

"Well. You know how it is." I balance my hands up and down in the air. "Catch waves. Plan for my future. Catch waves. Plan for my future."

Mr. Parker nods. "I didn't know you had drive, other than surfing. Maybe you can rub off on Grace. She's flaking out on picking a college." He extends his hand. We shake. "Good to have you on the team. I was impressed by your resumé. You have a lot to offer, son."

Wow. My eyes widen. "Thanks, sir."

"Meet your fellow partners in Copy Machine—Brianna and Hop."

Embarrassed, I wave at them both. Brianna gives me a look that says she's not impressed and eyes my pit stains. Hop smiles and nods once.

Mr. Parker says, "Take a seat. And today is the first and last day you'll be late. I don't do late. Neither do my interns. There are no free rides here—for anyone."

Bossman letting me know what's up. I can respect that. I don't ask for free rides or favors. I say, "Yes sir."

I slide into the seat between Hop and the beautiful Brianna. She scoots her chair away a couple of inches. Little Miss Subtle.

He flicks out his wrist and checks his watch. "I've got a meeting with a new client soon. Teresa will set you up with a tour of the place." He gives everyone a huge grin. "There were lots of applicants. The partners and I sifted through several strong resumés to come up with the best interns— the three of you. Don't disappoint me now." Then he walks to the door and turns around. "Ford, walk down the hall with me. You can join your cohorts for the tour in a couple of minutes."

I speed over to the doorway and catch up with him. "Sir, I'm really sorry about being late. It won't happen again."

He says, "No worries. I'm sure it won't."

We speed-walk past a few more conference rooms and then he enters his office. I follow him, feeling queasy.

He sits down behind his glass desk but doesn't motion for me to sit. "Well, I'm sure you're wondering what this is all about."

I nod. "Yes sir."

"Well, son, it's like this. The way I see it, your internship here turned out to be serendipity for both of us. You see, I know how you kids get all excited about senior year and call it senioritis, when it's really a bunch of kids sticking their middle fingers up at the world. Hell, I did it. But Grace needs to keep her focus. She's got a great shot at nailing valedictorian this year and she doesn't need any distractions. Her mother and I want what's best for her. The Ivy Leagues." He pauses and stares me down. I gulp. He continues. "I don't have to tell you how important things—like the right internship, the right connections, or the right school—can change someone's life."

I nod. He's right. It's the reason I'm standing in his office wondering what he's getting at. "Yes sir."

He smiles and bangs his fist on the desk. "I knew you'd get it. This is perfect. You're her best friend and surfing buddy. I need you to run recon for me. Keep those guys away from her. The last thing Grace needs is some sappy summer romance messing with her head. She needs to go into the school year ready to focus on academics."

Whoa. Are you kidding me? Dating Grace was my number-one goal for the summer ... and it's now in direct conflict with my number-two goal. It took me two years to work up the nerve to go after Grace, and now, in the span of a week, she's shot me down with the friend card and her dad, my new boss, is asking me to keep guys away from her. Rip my heart out already.

He waves his hand at me like no biggie. "Don't worry, Ford. You can do this, and I never ask for favors if I don't plan on returning them. You come through for me, I'm sure I can secure you an internship at Gutierrez, Haverty, and Mierl. That would be a great experience to have next summer, right before college. You've heard of them, right?"

Holy crap. Who hasn't? I suck in my breath. My head's reeling as I mentally run through the repercussions of saying no to my boss on the first day of work, saying no to the father of the girl I want to date, and possibly betraying my best friend who I want to date more than anything.

"Yes sir," I say. "They won a breakthrough case on immigration reform in California."

Mr. Parker nods. "Well, Miguel happens to be a good friend of mine. You watch out for my baby girl, and I'll take care of you. Deal?"

It's mainly for the summer, right? I think I could win over her dad by the school year, convince him I wouldn't be a distraction to Grace. As for the summer, Grace already shot me down anyway. And she's not into dating anyone right now, so it's not even like I'd be working against her—it's more like I'd be helping her maintain her goals, and those just happen to coincide with her dad's concerns. So, really, I'm not betraying anyone. I can do this, right? I tap my fingers on my leg. I can try again with Grace in the fall. What's a few extra weeks?

Besides, it's not like I have any great backup options. I say, "Deal."

"I knew I could count on you," Mr. Parker says. "Head on out to the copy machine tour."

I run down the hall and catch up with Brianna and Hop. They're still in Conference Room G, waiting for the tour.

Brianna looks at me, one eyebrow almost arched to her hairline. "What was that about? Found the strongest applicants to make copies?" She waves her arms around wildly, pointing toward me and Hop. "Are you kidding me? We've got a rainbow in here. Where's the token white kid?" She pops up out of her chair and her hands move automatically to her curvy hips. "And I'm not sticking around to make copies for the next eight weeks."

Wow, the girl's got fire. Wondering which question to answer, I shrug. "I'm half-white. Does that work for you?"

Hop laughs nervously. "Listen, you can take the all-righteous, too-good-for-everybody route *or* you can dig up the courage to stick it out. There's no way all we're going to learn is how to make copies. I don't know about you, but I sure could use a great letter of rec."

Brianna's going to murder Hop and I'm the key witness. He keeps his cool, waiting out her stare of death.

She says, "I've got game."

He shrugs. "I guess we'll see. Are you here to play the game? Or are you just here to be loud and make a big splash and a big exit?"

Daaaaamn! I laugh out loud. Couldn't help it. She directs her fierce gaze at me. I laugh again. "Nice try. I got a mama straight from Mexico. You haven't had the years of practice *or* the fire to come close to the looks my Ma shoots me."

She bristles like a cat rubbed the wrong way.

I shrug. "Just stating the facts. You got game or what? I'm going to get a tour of the copy machines from *Teresa*." I say "Teresa" with the Spanish accent.

Hop stands up and sticks out his fist. We bump fists over, under, and straight on. Then we walk out the door.

A few feet down the hall, I turn around. No Brianna. "Dude, you think she's gonna quit?"

Hop says, "No way. She's smarter than that. I called her

bluff. She needs a few minutes. Then she'll be here all summer to terrorize us with her awesome hot self."

We keep on walking.

Hop says, "You play poker?"

"Not really. I've been trying to spend time volunteering with organizations that help immigrants get legal status. I'm interested in immigration law." Not wanting to sound too serious or uptight, I shrug and add, "Well, that and surfing."

He claps his hands together and rubs them maniacally. "Awesome. I have a project of sorts that I need a little help with. You need to meet my crew—some of them could use your help. As for poker, we play for quarters."

We reach Teresa's desk without Brianna. Teresa's an uptight woman; I can tell that by looking at her. She dresses about ten years older than she is, and not in a good way. That dark black hair of hers is captured in a tight bun and she wears granny glasses. What's up with women who do that?

Teresa glances at us and points to nearby seats. No words. Then she looks back. "Where's Brianna?"

Hop says, "I think she had to powder her nose or something."

Teresa nods. We sit. A few minutes later Brianna huffs around the corner and sits next to me. Man, she's furious *and* she smells good.

———————

It turns out Teresa wasn't the one to give us a tour of the copy rooms. They got Jada for that. She's the head honcho of the mailroom and the copy brigade. Looking at her, she seems like a cool chick—a nose ring, little tatt on the back of her neck peeking above her collar, blond hair in a pony-tail. *Aw*, ponytails. But nope. She's a freakin' drill sergeant.

Once we've finished the driest tour in the history of intern-ships, I'm wondering about how bad I want that letter of rec-ommendation. The surf report today was decent—for sum-mertime. Grace probably caught a ride to the beach with someone else. Five bucks says it was a guy, and I bet Damien was eager to help out.

And the worst part about today? Brianna's running the copy machine while Hop and I watch.

Hop says, "Man, I never realized how much the art of making copies is like construction."

Brianna rolls her eyes.

He keeps going. "I guess every good copy project has one guy working and two supervising."

I laugh. "Good one, dude." Hop has a future career as a bad comedian.

Brianna focuses on that copier like it's delivering babies instead of papers.

I say, "Brianna—Let's pick up the pace. I need to see some more enthusiasm. Hop to it."

Hop says, "Dude, don't take my name in vain."

Brianna whips her head toward us and raises one eye-brow. "One, I don't need supervision, and two, you two fools couldn't handle me if you tried."

I like the way she thinks. In lists. And she's got *fuego*.

Hop keeps a straight face and turns to me. "The sign of a good handler is to corral the subject in a way that the subject does not know they've been handled." Then he looks at Brianna and says, "You stayed, didn't you? Between that and the fact that I've yet to lift a finger, I'd say I won this round hands down."

Burn.

Brianna's speechless mad.

Hop speaks into an imaginary microphone. "Come on, Brianna. Let's start over. I'm Hop. Vietnamese joker. I play poker. And I like to pick on hot chicks."

Girl's trying to stay mad, but it looks like Hop helped wear her down. He passes the mic to me. I grab it. "My name's Ford, not Ferdinand. I like water better than land. I like to surf, and..." Shoot. I'm stuck. "And you smell good?"

Brianna cracks a small smile.

"C'mon," I say. "Why can't we all get along? *We are the world* and all that. Besides, we didn't want you to leave this morning. You think I want to be stuck with a smelly guy who tells bad jokes all summer?"

Hop says, "Bad jokes maybe. You got the market *cornered* on smell. Bro, you need to invest in some mega antiperspirant."

"Brah, I am wearing it. I got stuck in traffic and had to run down fifty flights of stairs in the parking garage. Otherwise, I would have been later."

Brianna says, "Next time, be later."

"Ouch. It's not that bad."

Hop and Brianna look at each other and then say, "Yeah, it is."

"Dang. Well, if that's what it takes to bring people to-gether..." I shrug. "A guy's gotta do what a guy's gotta do. I'm all about saving the world, one stanky situation at a time."

five

It's awesome that I'm actually sitting on Huntington Beach watching a surf comp live. This is it. The place where surf history on the West Coast started. The place where guys like Duke Kahanamoku and Corky Carroll surfed, the beach that the USA surf team calls home. It's the quintessential spot to visit, a place where surfing isn't just a person on a board—it's a spiritual experience.

Sponsors bustle around getting things ready for the Surfer Girl Jr. Pro. They have tents everywhere, advertising everything from energy drinks to surf gear to sunscreen. As far as the actual competitors, they have their own area: a raised platform topped off by a big white canvas tent. Being here to watch a surf comp live is so freaking cool.

The drive here from San Diego only took an hour and a half, but even that short of a distance from my family can make a world of difference in my stress level. It's so awesome of Ford's uncle to let us stay at his beach house—Mama Watson said her brother's decorating taste is impeccable. I can't wait to see the place, but I'm definitely glad they dropped me and Ford off at the beach first, while they ran errands.

A weekend with the Watson family is my *get out of jail free* card. If it weren't for a breakthrough in one of Dad's cases (translation: I caught him in a good mood), I'd be at home dusting. If I believed in fate, maybe I'd look for some deep meaning, but I don't. I'll take what I can get. I relax and enjoy the comp set-up while Ford, practically salivating, runs around from tent to tent, checking out all the sponsors and perhaps a few girls.

After some time scoping things out, Ford jogs toward me looking like he belongs on some sort of commercial rather than just running toward a wanna-be surfer girl. He plops down on the sand next to me and waves a blue flyer in front of my face.

"Check it, *mamacita*." He places it between two of my toes like they're placeholders.

I grab the blue paper. "There's a new surf shop opening on the strip."

"Keep reading."

I scan down the page. "Holy crap. Holy crap. Holy—"

"Crap." Ford laughs. "That's right. In August, you're entering Crazy John's Surf Comp. His first annual. This is it—the break you've been looking for. Kickin' butt and taking names."

Speechless. Overload.

Ford says, "That's not all. I met the owner of the shop. Guess who one of the judges is?"

I squeak out, "Who?"

"The UC San Diego surf coach himself."

My chance. To go for it. To catch the coach's eye. To focus on all the moves I need to perfect.

Ford pats my leg. "Earth to Grace."

"I'm freaking out."

Ford laugh-cackles. "Heck yeah."

I shake my head side to side. "Not cool. I need some sort of way to get that guy's attention. Like pulling better moves. Not to mention my main ride to the beach is now interning at a law firm for the next seven weeks. I don't even know if I'll have the beach time to train and prove I can kick ass."

"Grace, you will. And you already kick butt. You just don't know it yet."

"What's that supposed to mean?"

Ford says, "It means you hold back. You don't fully give yourself to the move."

I toss the flyer between us. "Are you charging for this psycho-babble?"

"Nah. Call it a freebie, 'cause that's how I roll." He waggles his brows up and down. "Now for a little CYA. If you tell your folks about this comp thing... let's keep me out of the equation. Personally, I think it will be a great way to keep you focused on some fun this summer when you aren't doing all the college app stuff. Then, when school starts, you'll have kicked major butt at the surf comp and you'll be two hundred percent ready to kick butt all the way to your valedictorian speech next May."

Grinning at his need to cover his ass now that he works for my dad, I shrug and say, "When do I sign up?"

"Today. This is your chance. C'mon. Where's the thanks? The *you're my hero*?"

I lighten my voice and wrap my fingers around the sides of my feet. "Thanks, Ford. Really. You rock. So we're really going to sign up today?"

He eyes me and grins. "That's a start. *We're* not signing up, just you. You're the one that wants to make the UCSD surf team. Me? I've got an internship *con su padre*. Hardcore competing isn't my thing. It's yours. When it comes to surfing, I want it to be all about me and the ride. Nobody else."

I bite my lip. It must be nice for him, not feeling the need to compete. Just to be. Something deep down inside me says I have to fight harder than everyone else, because... well, because my world is so screwed up. And while part of me thinks their world is screwed up, too, another part of me says, not as much as mine.

My attention shifts. A flurry of activity in the competitors' tent gives me the impression the first heat will start soon. The first four competitors in the Surfer Girl Jr. Pro, wearing jerseys with their numbers on them, are checking into the ready area, where some super-tan guy with a visor gives them instructions. My stomach's doing sympathetic flip-flops. That's going to be me in two and half months? Gulp.

They're fidgeting back and forth, and the shortest girl keeps glancing at the ocean. Visor Guy's mouth moves a few more times and then he nods for them to paddle out. They catch a current and by the time they're at the designated area, the horn blares, signaling the start of their twenty-minute heat.

I curl my toes and tighten my fists as I consider the realities of competing. Judges score each contestant's top two waves based on the number of maneuvers and their respective difficulty, the surfer's control, and how the surfer maximizes the critical part of the wave. Only one contestant from each heat advances to the next round. No pressure, right?

The tallest girl catches the first wave and pulls a few cutbacks. No biggie, but then, holy crap! Un-freaking-believable—she executes a perfect 360. The crowd's going nuts. Um, hello. She just let everyone know she's not here to play. I've never seen a regular girl pull that move. That was epic. And I know, in every particle of my being, that it's the move I need to pull off.

After a glorious parent-free day, we walk a few blocks to the beach house. It's almost more like we're floating. Real life is a vague memory.

"Do you really think I can get there by August? Or am I going to look like a kook?"

Ford takes his empty Shaved Ice cup and hook-shots it into a trash can we pass. "Are you serious? You can do almost

47

every move we saw today. You just need to tweak them so they're bigger and sharper. You gotta showboat it, you know?"

"Maybe. But what about the 360? I've never even tried that move. And airs? I'm lucky to catch a little air action when I exit a ride."

"No sweat. We'll work on it. I'll be your personal coach—on the days I'm not working."

I think about that and crunch on another bite of coconut ice.

"If you're hesitating over fees, don't worry. I'm free." He reaches over and guides my hand so that I feed him my next bite.

"Hey! You should've gotten a larger size."

"Well, now I owe you. That seals the deal. You're going to kick ass, thanks to good old Coach Ford. Then you'll owe me for life."

"Bahaha. Yeah, right. Thanks for offering to help me train."

He takes my cup and says, "Consider this a down payment." Then he bolts around the corner.

I chase after him, half-panting, half-screeching, "Hey! You better not finish that ... I backwashed."

He laughs and sprints toward a large stucco beach house. He waits on the front porch, holding the cup as high in the air as he can. I jump and swipe at his arm. He laughs and hands it over.

Truth is, I like chasing after Ford and roughhousing. Not that I'd say it out loud. I tilt back my head and tap the last of the coconut-flavored ice into my mouth.

Ford opens the door with a sweeping gesture and waits for me to go in first. I walk in and immediately check out the beach house. It has some of my favorite beach colors—teal and espresso. This place freaking rocks.

His mom stands up from a white leather couch and walks toward us. His dad sits there quietly, waves at us, and goes back to perusing a car magazine.

"I'll give you the nickel tour." Ford nudges me. "We'll be sharing a room."

Mama Watson steps in between us and places her arm around Ford. "*Mijo*, you failed to mention that you'll be in separate beds on opposite sides of the room. And besides, the two of you are like cousins."

He ducks his head. "C'mon. It's me and Grace. Enough said." She gives him a playful whack and heads off down the hall.

He flexes his arm muscle, sporting a cheesy grin, and then runs up carpeted stairs, skipping every other one.

I roll my eyes. "I'm embarrassed for you. Really, I am." Then I follow, wondering what this weekend holds in store for me.

Ford leads me into the kids' room on the second floor. It has six built-in bunk beds lining the walls, three on each side. Every bed has its own privacy curtain and a lighted wall sconce for late-night reading, I guess. Umm—I think I'll manage to survive. Happy candy-pink and bamboo-green stripes accent the right side of the room, and bright blue and bamboo-green stripes accent the left side. The two sides are mirror images, furniture and all. I place my backpack against the wall by the last bed on the girls' side, which is next to a window.

Ford drops his bag in front of the bed directly across from mine. Only fifteen feet of floor space will separate us. We'll be in the same room with basically no adult supervision? Scratch that thought. Not going there. It's cool that his parents trust us, and it's not like we'd do anything, but it's weird. Here's the cookie jar; don't eat the cookies.

Ford clears his throat. "There's not really a view of the beach from this level. You have to be on the third story to get the views, which is where the adults stay. There's two master suites up there with their own private balconies, so my uncle and whatever friends he brings can all have their privacy."

"Wow."

Ford swipes at his hair. "Yeah, it's pretty cool. My uncle's an architect, so he's definitely into details. If you want, we could hit the roof and check out the sunset. Maybe I'll even share a deep dark secret."

Like Ford has any deep dark secrets. Ha, he doesn't know dark.

"You're so funny." I plop down on a beige beanbag and kick off my flip-flops.

It's amazing to spend a weekend away from home. But I hope Ford won't try to make a move, as much as it makes me tingle all the way down to my toes. This summer is dedicated to surfing and figuring out how to make it into UCSD through a surf scholarship. I can't handle any more messy relationships. My family's stocked up on that score. Besides, I've never even dated anybody. Too busy making the grades and not really interested in something that will only end up in a break-up. Because I swear, the first time a boyfriend hits me? I'm out of there.

———————

At bedtime, we take turns getting ready in the bathroom. Ford lets me go first and hangs out in our room while he waits. Awkward … I hesitate before coming out in a blue tank top and blue-and-green-plaid PJ shorts. Ford smiles suggestively at me; I feel like he's scoping out every detail.

I thump him on the head and mimic his earlier statement, "C'mon. It's me, Grace."

He drops to his knees and says, "A thousand pardons, my lady. If I'd known how hot you looked in your night-time attire, I wouldn't have made such rash promises to my dear mother."

I reach out to thump him again and he catches my arm and pulls me toward him. Harder than he meant to, I guess, because I fly at him and we topple on the floor, a tangle of arms and legs. I roll off of his chest and we lie next to each other, laughing.

After a few minutes, I say, "You're nuts."

"That's why we hang out."

"Because you're certifiably insane?"

He gets up and turns back to face me before shutting the bathroom door. "Because I, dear Grace, am your comic relief."

I walk over to the bed replaying flashes of what happened

over in my head. Ford is more than comic relief. He's every-thing—escape, fun, comfort, encouragement, and a million other things. He's my security blanket. It makes me feel like a two-year-old, but that's the truth. When I'm around him, I feel like I'm who I could be all the time.

I flounce onto the bed and space out until the click of the bathroom door opening announces his presence. He comes out wearing a towel wrapped around his waist. My jaw drops. He howls with laughter and whips it off, reveal-ing knee-length basketball shorts. I toss a pillow at him, which he catches.

"Parker, don't get in over your head. Besides, you owe me an apology for ogling."

"Was not."

"Were too."

"Whatev."

He tosses the pillow back. "Sweet dreams."

I place it on my bed and slide under the covers. "Yeah, you too."

He turns on a nightlight and flips out the main light, then he runs full speed at his bed, bouncing onto it at the last possible second.

I nibble at my lip and wonder how in the world I'll fall asleep. "G'night."

"G'night."

I adjust the covers, making sure my arms are out. This entire day passed without any major stress—I didn't feel like I was floating in a barrel headed toward Niagara Falls. Riding to the beach with his parents was actually fun.

Even though Mr. Watson's speed-racing stressed out Mama Watson, who would screech "Eli" in a high-pitched voice whenever she wasn't muttering Hail Mary's, there was never tension or doubt that they loved each other—which totally makes me think how my parents are the complete opposite. At least, it seems that way.

This is the last thing I want to think about, here in this stress-free zone, but I can't help it. My stomach starts hurting a little and I can feel the acid churning in there. What is wrong with me? I need to calm down, relax. Breathe deep and all that crap. But no amount of breathing can stop the wheels from turning inside my mind.

Fragmented images fly through my head—some fun, some scary. Surfing at the beach, Dad's face when he's angry, shopping, jogging in the park with Mom, Mom lecturing me on making a good impression, wearing clothes I don't like, working out with Ford. Then come the big fears. The possibility of having surfing taken away if I screw up in school and lose my class rank. Not knowing when Dad's going to explode. Whether or not I will be able to bring it to the Crazy John's Surf Comp. It's like being on an out-of-control tilt-a-whirl at a carnival. Even on a dream weekend, I can't escape the stress of home.

I wonder what Ford's thinking about.

I whisper, "You awake?"

"Yeah."

"Wanna talk?"

His bed creaks as he rolls over. "If you do."

I hesitate and then whisper-yell, "Incoming!" I stifle a

laugh as best I can, already feeling my back muscles loosening up as I grab a beanbag chair and tiptoe-run to his bed. If his mom comes in we're toast, but I don't care. I want to be near him. I want to be safe.

He scoots over and pulls back the covers. "Don't worry. I sleep naked."

"Ew."

"Kidding, Parker."

I throw the beanbag next to me at the end of his bed and sit cross-legged, nervous about being so close to him and aching to be held.

He gets up, grabs the beanbag from beside me, and sets it onto the floor against the side of the bed. Then he swoops me down onto the beanbag with him. His arm around my waist, with just my pajamas between us, makes me shiver. In one quick swoop, he grabs the blanket off his bed and tucks it around me. I pull my arms out on top, needing that freedom—that control.

I croak, "Thanks."

He clears his throat. "Yeah, sure. But don't go thinking I'm easy. You know how it is these days. Word gets around that a guy's easy and he becomes nothing more than a target to nail. You girls can be so shallow. A girl gets some and she's a hero, a guy gets some and he's a slut."

I lean against him, playfully. "Ha ha."

The inch between our bodies radiates with heat. If I move the slightest bit, his naked chest will be against my arm. He half turns on his side to face me, and the gap between us widens ever so slightly. Mirroring him, I roll onto my side, folded on the beanbag, unsure of what to do—hovering so close to the edge I could tumble off. Ford's more than just a guy. He's oxygen when I can't breathe. Being this close relaxes me; I breathe a little deeper, taking in his soapy scent, holding on to anything good. I reach out and lay my arm in the middle of the space between us. He tilts his head and we lock eyes. I nibble my upper lip. He brushes his thumb across my mouth and says, "Don't bite your lips, they'll get chapped."

A shiver runs through me and I wonder if this is real or not. I bite my lip again, and smile at the involuntary action. He smiles back and plants his hands in his lap, like he's willing them to behave.

Ford says, "What's going on? What's important enough to risk *The Wrath of Mama Watson?*"

I stare at the shape of his fingernails; they're wide and strong like his hands. He could engulf my hands with his big brown paws. "I don't know. Stuff. Senior year. Class rank. The Parentals freak out about dumb stuff."

"Dude, it's summer. Don't stress early. And welcome to the club. Lots of parents freak out over dumb stuff, especially senior year."

"Yeah, right. I can so see your perfect parents blowing up."

"Nobody's parents are perfect. Everyone has issues."

I snort. "Some more than others. What kinds of issues go on in your family? Your mom gets diagnosed with the messy absentminded-professor syndrome?"

"Uncool," Ford says. "You're not the only person in the world entitled to problems."

I touch his hand. "Sorry. What are your parents freaking out over?"

"It's not so much that my parents are freaking out. I put enough pressure on myself." There's a long pause as he glances down and fidgets with his hands. "This internship at your dad's firm is important. It's part of my resumé." He scoots an inch away and pulls back while he looks me in the eyes. "I gotta be careful, make sure I don't screw it all up."

He's so driven. He knows what he wants and goes for it. "What do you want to do? Really?" I ask.

Ford shrugs. "The only thing I want right now is to surf and hang out with you. Unless you wanna talk about your crap, let's chill."

Why won't he talk about himself? But I just say, "Can I stay over here a little longer?"

He burrows into the beanbag and pulls me to him. "Yeah, it's not like we're doing anything . . . you know what I mean."

I do. He's totally making sure I know he's not hitting on me. He's such a sweetheart. I fold into him, feeling his warmth against me. My chest is brushing his, my hips are leaning into him; I tentatively lay my arm across his middle, snuggling into him, relaxing as he cradles me, and letting go of anything but the thought of him. I drift off, thinking *finally, peace*.

six

moon cakes: *a pastry associated with the moon festival celebrated by the Chinese, Taiwanese, and Vietnamese in mid-autumn, usually filled with meats or sweets*

I walk into the office building ten minutes early. Week two. Day four. My mission: wear Teresa down and get some dirt on the real work, something more than copying papers. Doing that for the next seven weeks with Hop and Brianna? Somebody ain't coming out of that alive, and I put my money on Brianna being one of the two survivors.

I jog up the stairs, open a glass door, and enter Teresa's lair ... whistling.

She looks up from her desk, glasses perched on her nose like an old lady. She's not *that* old, but she's not as young as Jada. I'm guessing mid-thirties to forties.

I say, "*Buenos dias.*"

She half frowns. "Good morning."

I walk toward her, hands in my pockets. "I thought you spoke Spanish?"

She says, "Not unless I'm translating."

I press on. "*¿Porque?*"

She pushes her glasses up and looks around. "And who would I be speaking Spanish with? I answer phones and make appointments."

I lean against her desk, smiling like she gave me the biggest compliment in the world. "Oh Terrrrresa." Totally rolled that R, extra. She seems embarrassed to embrace her Latina side in this law office, which is really odd. Being bilingual is awesome. I'll win her over. Before long, she'll be making me *tortas con carne* and saying, "*¿Que paso?*"

After a quick knock on her desk, I wink. "C'mon. You run this place. What's the scoop? How does an intern get to do more than make copies? Besides—you can speak a little *español* with me." I look around conspiratorially. Then I whisper, "I won't tell. Cross *mi corazon*."

She fights a smile and waves me away. "It's a good thing you're early today."

I back away from her desk and bow. "Only *para ti*."

She waves me away, but her cheeks are red.

I sit down and say, "Nice glasses. Kind of hipsterish."

She types furiously on her keyboard. "*Gracias*. And you might talk to Jada. There's an immigration case they've taken on and all the paralegals and admins are going nuts trying to keep up with the caseload, which means you might get to do something besides make copies."

Aw, yeah. I smile wide. "*¿Que?*"

She says, "You heard me."

"Yeah. I heard you."

Teresa adjusts her headset and gets back to typing.

Brianna walks in looking like a Banana Republic model. And while it's not free-spirited hippie-girl clothes, she's looking good. But I like Grace's look better. And even though I'm surrounded by hot girls all summer, they don't hold a candle to Grace. An office romance would have nothing on our middle-of-the-night beanbag tryst. But there's nothing wrong with a little innocent flirting—I've never been one to ignore a pretty girl.

She gives me a slight nod and takes a seat a couple chairs down from me.

I laugh and smell my pits. "I swear I doubled up today. Really." Then I pat the chair next to me.

Brianna rolls her eyes and shakes her head. "Where's your pride?"

I shrug. "Lost. With my ego?"

She picks at imaginary lint. "I doubt that."

A slight bit of guilt crosses over me as I think of Grace. But what am I supposed to do? She's off-limits. I gulp down the ache in my throat. I need to get focused on my own priorities, and that includes making a difference, not copies.

The door opens and in walks Hop.

Teresa says, "Barely on time."

Hop looks at the clock. "One minute to spare. Crazies on the bus this morning."

Now that Hop's here, I'm ready to break the news about our potential lucky break.

Teresa says, "You may go to Jada's office and get your assignment for the morning."

Brianna mutters, "Great. More copies."

"Why such a limited vision?" Hop asks. "We might graduate to filing paperwork."

Teresa grunts. "Fat chance."

I walk down the hall, whispering to Hop and Brianna about the immigration case and how we have an angle on getting to do something worthwhile this summer.

I walk into Jada's territory, words rolling around in my head as I wonder how to get us in on some real legal action. The tension hangs in the air like San Francisco fog.

Well, here goes. "Good morning, Jada."

She glances up from behind a mountain of boxes, her tiny diamond nose ring the only thing decorating her otherwise frustrated face.

"What?" I joke. "Are they trying to bring new meaning to the phrase *buried in paperwork*?"

She glares.

I throw my hands up in the air in surrender. "*Ai*. Sorry. Really. It looks like a ridiculous amount of stuff to process and sort."

Jada flicks a piece of lint off her skirt. "No shit, Sherlock."

I pat one of the boxes. "Listen, I know we're newbs, but we're not at the top of our class for nothing. I swear we could help you tear through this pretty fast and we won't screw up." I turn around to Brianna and Hop. "Right?"

Brianna steps forward and says, "He's right. Just tell us what to do and we'll ace it for you."

Jada scans the three of us like she's trying to decide if we're for real. Then she points to a box and says, "Some of those files still need to be stamped for receiving. Date's on the Post-it. Screw it up and somebody gets the axe, and it won't be me. Ford, you stamp. Brianna and Hop, I'm going to show you how to sort and label."

———————

Hop talks non-stop the entire drive to his apartment. Dude talks more than most girls. Good thing he's funny.

Before turning into his lot, I ask, "So, do I need to park on the street? What's the deal with guests?"

Hop laughs. "Who said you were a guest? That kind of thinking might make me feel a little sorry when I take all your money."

I snort. "Ha. Where do I park?"

"You can park in our spot, 1412 A. The neighbors might think we got a vehicle."

I turn in and cut the engine. Esmerelda's cough sputters.

Hop says, "Whoa, dude. We've got standards." He pats the dash. "She might make us look bad with her crankiness."

The apartment building is kind of a dump on the outside. Hop's got a good sense of humor—my truck looks at home here. I step outside and enjoy the image of Hop struggling to open the passenger door.

When he finally barrels out, much like Grace does, he

says, "What I lack in muscle, I make up for in cunning. How else do you think my skinny ass survived this part of town for sixteen years?"

I double-take. "Sixteen? I thought you were a senior."

He shrugs, sheepish. "I am. Let's go check out Mom's latest and greatest."

The key sticks when Hop tries to unlock his front door. He jiggles the key and lifts the door to get in. A little WD40 would fix that. I'll bring some with me next poker night.

We walk into a small, immaculate apartment. The living and dining rooms are kind of combined into one. The perfect bachelor pad. You can see their kitchen from the front door. And the smells coming out of that oven make me want to cry.

I say, "Dude, this could be my second home."

Hop grins appreciatively. "Wait until you taste it. Mom works at Bountiful Moon bakery."

"I'm their newest customer."

"Tell 'em Hop sent you."

His mom walks in from the hallway.

"Hey," Hop says. "These moon cakes for poker night?"

She nods and her eyes lighten. "Suzhou are on the counter. New recipe in oven. Chocolate nut fruit."

Hop gives his mom a big squeeze. "You rock. Thanks."

Her eyes widen. She nods at me. "You must be Hop's friend from work."

I step forward and shake the hair out of my eyes. "Yes, ma'am. I'm Ford. It's nice to meet you."

"I am Mrs. Liang. Nice to meet you. You like moon cakes?"

I take in a deep breath and close my eyes. Then I open them. "I love them."

"Good." She looks at Hop. "Make sure your friend get enough to eat. Extra Suzhou. He growing boy."

I like the way she thinks.

Hop says, "Yes ma'am."

"You boys don't get too loud this night. You know Mrs. Tan will complain rest of week at Laundromat."

Hop rolls his eyes. "Mrs. Tan can—"

"Say what she like," Mrs. Liang says. "Watch the noise." Oh man. The Look is definitely universal.

Hop backs down fast. "Yes ma'am."

Then Mrs. Liang goes back into her room and closes the door. A minute later, the sounds of a sewing machine fill the space she left.

I look at Hop. "Dude, your mom has you whipped."

He shrugs. "And your mom doesn't?"

I grin. "Ma's from Mexico. What do you think?"

He grins. "Want a moon cake?"

"You know it. What's Suzhou?"

He grabs some plates and stacks a few moon cakes on them. "My favorite. They're made from pork. Mom adds some kick to hers. Hope you can handle the heat."

I grab the plate out of his hands. "Handle the heat? Ma's mole sauce will make a man beg for mercy. When do the guys get here?"

Hop's face turns serious. "About that. One of my friends needs—"

63

The doorbell rings. Hop shouts, "We already started loading up on the moon cakes."

The door flies open. A short Asian kid decked out like a pimp stands in the doorway, complete with dark glasses and gold chains. "What's up, yo?"

Then he strides over to the bar and loads up a plate. He gives me a side glance and does the head nod.

I say, "'Sup?"

Hop balls up a paper towel and pegs Future Pimp in the head. "Leave some for the rest of the guys, Hien."

Hien doesn't blink an eye. He joins us at the table.

Hop says, "Nobody told Hien he's Asian. He's had an identity crisis since elementary when he moved here."

Hien takes a big bite and says, "Yeah, and Hop's sucked at poker since we started this weekly gig. You don't see me complaining. He keeps me supplied with bling, yo."

I shove a moon cake in my mouth so I don't laugh at this little hip-hop dude.

Hop says, "Yeah, yeah. Where's the rest of the crew?"

"Ah dude, they be helping the latest FOB figure out the bus system. They'll be here any minute."

Hop nods.

"FOB?" I ask.

Hien tucks a large bite in his cheek. "Fresh Off the Boat. As in still not speaking the English well."

"Oh."

Hop says, "Our group...we take them in until they get things figured out. And Hien, here, he's our non-example of how to fit in."

I think about Jorge and ask, "Are these FOBs legal?"

Hien narrows his eyes. "You legal?"

I lean back. "Totally didn't mean it that way dude. I just wondered if I could help, you know?"

Hop pelts Hien with the paper towel right between the eyes. "He wants to go into immigration law. Help people not get deported, yo."

Hien wads the paper towel and throws it back at Hop. "Yeah, well, you never know."

Jorge's face floats through my mind. I can't let it go. "They have a place to go? You know, like use computers. Learn English. Find a lawyer?"

"Yeah," Little Hien says. "There's an Asian American Cultural Center that helps FOBs. But their computers suck." He shrugs. "Sometimes it's better to go to the library. Lawyers? They're for peeps with cash, bro."

I nod, thinking I bet Ma could get the university to donate some old computers to them. Ones that are only a year or so old.

The door flies open and three guys come in talking smack. They head straight for the moon cakes and help themselves. If Hien is a Future Pimp, the rest of these guys have futures in the computer or gaming industry.

Soon the game of poker begins. Texas Hold'em. I've seen this game on TV and played it a few times on the Internet.

I arrange my cards, then ask, "What's the ante?"

Hien says, "Twenty-five cents."

And so we're off. About halfway into the game, with

most of my money gone, Hien looks up at me and asks, "So how do you and Hop know each other?"

I toss out a quarter. "From our internship at Bristol and Wentworth."

"Internship?" Hien tugs his sunglasses down a bit and looks at Hop with one eyebrow raised.

Hop cracks his knuckles. Then he chimes back, "Hey, there are hot, styling babes where I work. Better than the catch at the lame-o movie theater."

Sunglasses shoot back up and Hien slouches into his chair. "Hey. I get you into free movies, so show some respect." He leans back into the table. "What kind of hot babes? You gonna hook a bro up?"

"You don't need a girl," Hop says. "You need status. The legal kind. I was thinking Ford and I might figure out a way to help."

He looks across the table at me. Jorge flashes through my mind again. I glance at Hien, who's sitting there tense behind his glasses, constantly rearranging his cards. My summer just took on a whole lot more meaning.

I swallow hard and say, "Sure, man. We got you covered."

seven

Out of the water, I am nothing.
—Duke Kahanamoku

Beads of water roll off Damien's dreads. A big set comes at us and he says, "All right, girl. Let's catch this one together. Just for fun."

I paddle hard. "I'm breaking left."

He's a few feet over and a bit behind me. "You got it, babe."

After this past weekend at Huntington, I knew I needed to get up the nerve to ask other guys for a ride to the beach. Damien was the one I felt the most comfortable asking. Since he gave me a lift, I guess we're kind of surf buddies for the day.

I watch as the wave crests and Damien gets sucked up in the sweet spot. I paddle hard and kick to catch it. Oh yeah. I drop in next to him and we surf next to each other for a few seconds before breaking different directions to carve down the line. I don't pull any fancy moves. Hanging out with Damien is chill, and it's fun front-porching it, but I know I need to get serious and work on my 360 even on the days I'm not surfing with Ford.

The wave fizzles out and I exit the ride.

Damien and I paddle back over to each other. Sure, he may rub Ford the wrong way, but I think that's a total guy thing.

I reach Damien and say, "So when are you going to teach me how to pull an air?"

He straddles his board, hands resting on the rails. "Me teach you moves? I thought you were teaching me."

I splash at him. "Oh come on. You know you pull sick airs."

He grins. "I might be persuaded to give you a few pointers."

This feels so flirty and fun. "And how does that work?"

"I pick you up tomorrow."

Tomorrow is Ford's day off. I say, "I already made plans."

"A girl in demand. I can respect that. What's the rest of your week looking like?"

I ponder, mull it over dramatically. "Friday?"

He flashes pearly whites. "Done, boss."

———

Damien drops me off after a sweet surf session. When I walk through the front door, Dad's sitting in the recliner with his lips curled in a scowl. Crap. I hate it when a case drives him so nuts that he seeks the refuge of our house. His safe zone equals me walking on eggshells. He looks ready for a fight. Fear flashes through me like lightning.

"Hey, Daddy." I try to sound upbeat. "Everything okay?"

He pops up out of his chair. "Where have you been all day? I've been worried sick." He greets me with a slap across the face.

I reel backward, shocked at the sting warming my cheek. I blink a couple of times, angry at the unexpectedness. His outbursts are always random, never logical. Even on the days when nothing happens, he still has the advantage because I never know what's going to set him off.

"I was surfing. Remember? I told you I'd be surfing." I fight the desire to cringe. Tears well up at the corners of my eyes. Furious, I bite down hard and stiffen my lips.

"Yeah, in the morning. Not all damn day. And what beach were you at?"

I put all my nervous energy into flicking my pointer finger over and under my thumb, hiding my fear. "We went to La Jolla. I thought I told you."

"Well, maybe you ought to write it down next time." His jaw muscles flex in and out. Clearly he's itching for a fight.

I clasp my hands into a fist to still my nerves. "Jeez. I'm really sorry, Dad."

The veins in his neck throb and his face flushes. "Jeez" was the wrong word choice. Shit.

My dad slaps me over and over as I run across the living room, playing dodge and retreat as best I can. When I reach my room, my escape route fails. He shoves me across my room. I land smack into my dresser, the metal handle jamming into my lower back.

"What were you thinking? Did you think you could get away with it? Surfing all day? Are you trying to dodge your chores?" The back of his hand is poised in the air—ready to strike.

"No, Daddy. I swear." A small sob escapes.

He tosses me onto my bed, knocking the mattress half off. I clench my wrought iron bedframe; fear courses through me. I have nowhere to run. I shrink back and flinch.

Instead of hitting me again, he stalks out of the room, damage complete.

Once he slams the door behind him, I crumple in a heap against my bedframe, cover my face, and sob without sound. Crying silently has been painfully acquired. My way of not letting him know how much he hurts me. My way of maintaining dignity. My way of pretending I'm tough. Nobody likes a whiner anyway. People ask how you're doing, but they don't want the real answer. They want the nice one. Your dad hits you? Forget it.

I think about another of Eleanor Roosevelt's famous quotes:

> *No one can make you feel inferior without your consent.*

When I regain my composure I practically tiptoe to the kitchen, knowing Dad is back in his office. Even so, I don't want to alert him to the fact that I'm out of my room.

I run the hot water in the sink until it's three quarters of the way full. My lower back aches—the dresser really nailed it. Then I wipe down the counters while the dishes soak, pausing every now and then to rub at my back or stretch the tight muscles out. I'm careful to dry the counters without leaving streaks. Once the dishwasher is loaded, I measure out the detergent, carefully.

Most people use too much detergent or not enough,
but Parkers use the right amount of stuff.—Dad

It's usually funny, except when it isn't.

I walk gently back to my room, hugging the wall, hoping not to be noticed. I pull out some college apps to make it look like I'm working on them. Then I leave Post-it notes all over the house, making certain my parents know my locale. I check myself in the mirror to make sure I don't have marks anywhere. Then I turn around and peek at my lower back. There's a bruise already forming. But I'm wearing a long T-shirt so it doesn't matter. I'll just have to be careful at the beach around Ford. The advantage of a wetsuit—it hides the marks.

I escape on my bike back to Ford's house. If I had a car like most kids my age, life would be so much easier. But my parents like control. Cars equal freedom. Therefore, Grace "is fortunate to have a bike to ride."

After spending the weekend with Ford's family, it feels like the right place to go. Fifteen minutes later, I skid into the Watson driveway. Mama Watson answers the front door when I knock.

"Grace? *Mija*, come here." She gives me a big hug and it's all I can do not to break down and tell her everything. She seems so warm and safe. I fight tears welling up at the corner of my eyes, trying desperately to pretend nothing's wrong, even though it's probably obvious from my puffy eyes that I've had a less-than-stellar day.

I sniffle. "Is Ford home?"

A look of concern crosses her face. She shakes her head. "No. He texted me something about going to Hop's for poker. He won't be home until late tonight."

My shoulders slump. I expected Ford to be here. Waiting for me. Not hanging out with new people from work. I feel sick. I should have texted. Why would I think that if he's not with me, he must be at home? He has a life...other friends. Unlike me.

Mama Watson says, "I know I'm no Ford. But do you want to talk over hot cocoa?"

"Oh, no. I'm okay. Thanks though."

She steps toward me, hesitantly. "I'm here if you change your mind."

I nod and get back on my bike. I pedal away from home base toward town, wondering where to go.

eight

royal flush: *the five highest cards of a suit where the ace ranks high; the best hand in certain games of poker*

My cell buzzes and I check my messages. Grace texted me:

> Breakfast on Dad this morning. Pick me up hungry.
> Treating you to fave coffee shop first.

I throw everything in my truck and head out. When I roll up Grace's drive, she's waiting on her front porch. Her norm. She's always so stoked about the waves she can't stand missing out on a minute. That's one of the things I love about Grace.

I leave Esmerelda running and play it cool walking up her driveway. She's walking toward me, bag over her shoulder. "Want me to grab your board?"

She nods and walks toward the truck. She never says yes

when I offer to grab her board. I jog over and grab it. Don't want to look too eager. Then I carry it under my arm and whistle as I head over to place it in the bed of my truck.

Grace stands by the passenger door. "So you gonna be a gentleman or what?"

I smile and hurry over to yank the door open, uncomfortable. This would have been cool before I made the Deal-with-the-Dad. She's throwing out all the signs. Heck, at this point she's gonna be asking me out. And then I'll be stuck between a rock and a hard place. She climbs up into Esmerelda and lets me close the door.

I trot to the driver's side 'cause I'm playing it cool. She looks good today. I shift into drive, figuring out how to joke this off. "So who is this demure sugar mama sitting next to me? Buying breakfast. Wanting doors opened. Were you abducted by aliens last night?"

"No. Poker players."

I laugh. "Yeah. Well, you'll be glad to know I was robbed. Of like five dollars in quarters. At one point I had twenty. But since fifteen of those buckeroonies were bonus, they don't count. These guys would crack you up, Grace. You should have seen them last night. You'd have thought I was hanging out with professional poker players. One dude even wore sunglasses the whole time. And kept a straight face."

Grace settles back into the seat. "Well, I'm glad you had fun with your new friends."

She sure as heck doesn't sound like it. I exit her neighborhood. "I can tell. Where to after coffee, Queen Grace?"

"Bagel Palace?"

Grace could care less where we eat before surfing. In fact, the quicker the better. So she's being extra sweet suggesting one of my favorite places, Bagel Palace, which can have major lines.

"You got it." I turn up the radio.

———

Breakfast at Bagel Palace shakes things back to normal. When we get to the beach, I carry our boards and Grace carries the bags. We reach our spot to set up camp. I lay the boards down. Grace tosses me wax and I get to work. She shimmies into her wetsuit and zips herself. That's weird. It's usually my job.

I say, "All right, Femme Fatale—you ready to bust a 360 or what?"

"I hope."

I toss her the wax. "Hope? What kind of talk is that?"

She shrugs.

"You gotta get out there and show the wave who's boss."

She grabs her board and turns around.

I go for it. "So, who you been surfing with this week?"

She says, "Damien's been giving me rides. He even gave me some nice pointers on airs."

Inwardly, I wince. The dude's a total douche and his reputation with the ladies isn't the kind of thing I want Grace involved with, and it's certainly not what Mr. Parker would want for her. Damien will just take what he can get and then walk away with her dignity and a smile. Freakin' A. What to do...

I zip my suit and then attach my leash. "Watch out for him. It's cool he's giving you pointers, but remember his reputation."

Grace huffs. "It's not—"

I back up and say, "I'd hate for you to get mixed up with that. Remember your focus: surfing and academics. Heartache's not on the list." As she opens her mouth to protest, I say, "Let's kick it."

Then I run into the water, shins splashing salt. She laughs and follows, too competitive not to race me. The best moment of the day so far. We paddle out to where everyone else is already catching waves. Grace lags behind.

An hour later, I've shredded waves. Grace has been shredded.

She paddles over to me looking tired and pissed. "C'-mon," I say. "Your last try was better. You sort of pulled a 200, if that's a move." Then, to lighten things up: "But I have to say—your wipeouts have style. The way your body angles toward the water as your board nosedives is impressive."

"What is this? A bad attempt at reverse psychology?"

I shrug. "If the board shorts fit..."

She squares her body and paddles toward an incoming set. In a rush to catch the wave, she hits it right and pulls a massive bottom turn before assaulting the lip. Her board goes vertical for an instant before she spins 180. And thar she blows. She bunks the rotation and crashes. A minute later she pops up to the surface sputtering.

I paddle over, grinning. Push her board over to her. She clings to it like moss on a rock. "You're da bomb, baby. Da bomb. You were so close. I totally thought you were going to nail it. Ready to get back in the saddle?"

Her cheeks puff up before she blows the air out. "I'm cashed."

I look over at the guys. "Did you hear that, Buzzy? She says she's cashed."

He spits and then runs his hand through his super-short blond hair, making saltwater spray off of it. He tilts his head and checks me out. "*Bull*shit."

Damien paddles closer. "*Hell* no she's not. She's just getting started. Hey, Grace. Good to see you out today. I didn't know you were going to make it."

Freaking interloper. But that was enough for Grace. Her ego can't take a double whammy. She puffs up like a little rooster, cheeks red. Good. She needs some fire. And what the hell was that about *didn't know you were going to make it*? What? Does Damien keep tabs on Grace now?

"C'mon. Let's show 'em what you got."

Grace paddles over to the lineup. Buzzy, Damien, and I follow. Party waves suck. There's a few kooks out here who don't know crap about the way things go down on crowded days. They better stay off my waves. A nice set barrels toward us about a hundred yards out.

I reach over and give Grace's board a pat, like I would my truck. "The waves are filthy. This is it. I can feel it. You're gonna go crazy on those waves and show folks how it's done."

Grace laughs and nods, kind of high-strung. She seems

off today; I don't get it. We paddle over to the spot where it should peak and wait. When it's go time, I give Grace's board a shove and say, "Paddle!"

Aw, crap. She dropped in on the wave at the same time as a newbie. Freakin' A. He's moving to cut her off. But Grace carves hardcore. She's not taking this—and then the jerk shoves her off her board.

Dude's going down.

I turn around, looking for some peeps. Buzzy. Sweet. I yell, "Did you see that shit?"

Buzzy looks toward the jerkoff riding straight down the line. What a waste of a wave. He says, "Hell yeah I did."

Damien paddles over like he can't get out of my business.

I head over toward Grace. She's not up yet. Panic fills me. I grab her board and tug on her leash. There's drag. She pops up to the surface.

I lean over, worried. "Why'd you stay under so long? That wigged me out."

She clenches her jaw, climbs on her board. She turns her back and tugs on her wetsuit. There's a small hole in her wetsuit, down low, at the small of her back.

"He sliced your wetsuit with his fin?" I turn toward Buzz and Damien and yell, "Somebody needs to take care of that chump. He ran over Grace with his fin. I'm gonna paddle in with her. Who's got dibs on kicking his ass outta here?"

Damien says, "I'll help him find his car."

Buzzy says, "Hell yeah."

"Don't beat him up," Grace says. "Okay?"

Damien frowns. Then he smiles and says, "How about

a firm suggestion? And then if he doesn't see reason . . . "

He holds his hands up. There's only so much a guy can do. This may be his only moment of redemption.

I give him a thumbs-up. I tell Grace, "Start paddling. You're probably bleeding in the water, and unless you want to attract any more sharks than you probably already have, I suggest you don't slow down until you hit the shore."

When we reach the shoreline, I flag down a lifeguard. She jogs over with her first aid kit.

The lifeguard asks, "Everything okay?"

I say, "Not so much. A moron ran over her with his board."

The lifeguard steps in closer. "Ouch. Could you pull down your suit for me and let me get a look at it?"

"Not until he's looking a different direction." Grace turns to me. A lot of emotions pass across her face, but I don't get any of them.

Unbelievable. I give her a *what's up with that* look, then I turn around, annoyed. Like, I've seen her tah tahs when a wave hit her suit the wrong way last August, and she doesn't want me to see the top inch of her butt? Really?

Then she grunts and I hear her unzip her suit by herself.

I peek around. She flinches, and it drives me nuts she's not letting me help her. That dude really knocked her around. I kind of hope Damien needs to provide a little extra persuasion to get him to leave. Never thought I'd be on the same side as him.

The lifeguard lets out a low whistle. "That's one hell of

a bruise. The cut's not too bad. At least you don't need any stitches."

I half turn and take a look. Damn. How'd she get the bruise? The lifeguard digs around in her first aid kit, then blocks my view with her body. Her arm is moving like she's wiping the cut. Grace doesn't make a sound.

Then the lifeguard pulls out a bandage.

I give Grace a thumbs-up. She bestows a tiny half smile.

The lifeguard applies the bandage. Then she says, "Wait a bit to make sure your cut isn't bleeding before you get back in the water. And take care of yourself. I'd say you've got enough injuries for the week."

Grace nods, cheeks red.

The lifeguard looks at Grace and then at me—hard—like I had something to do with the jerk-off running over her. She says, "You're sure you're okay?"

"Yeah," Grace says.

The lifeguard shrugs. "Take care of yourself."

I put my arm around Grace. "Don't worry. She's in good hands."

We walk over to the boards. Grace bends toward her board. I make a quick block.

She puts her hands on her hips. "I got a little cut on my butt, not my arms."

"You get five points for rhyming but that's not enough for me to allow you to carry your board, ma'am."

She raises a brow. "Cheap points."

"Cheap rhyme." I wink. "Take a load off. Those waves aren't going down anytime soon."

I take her hand, an electric moment, and pull her over to a beach towel. We plop down.

I say, "How'd you get the bruise on the top of your butt?"

She frowns. "How about respecting a girl's privacy? You weren't supposed to look."

"Temptation won."

She digs her toes in the sand, classic Grace. "I fall on my surfboard all the time, detective."

I tug her ponytail. "Well, maybe you need to be more careful, Womanista."

She shrugs and stares at the ocean. I watch her, waiting. Then she looks at me and smiles like nothing bad happened today. "Let's grab a snow cone—it's on my dad." She looks so cute as she holds her hand out for mine. I let her pull me up and we run over to the snow cone stand.

Thirty minutes later, we're in the party line. The guys give Grace mad props for coming back out.

Buzzy whistles. Then he says, "You really get sliced?"

I say, "Is the Pope Catholic? Yeah, she did."

Grace laughs.

"Girl, you're *boss*." Damien says. He puffs his chest and surveys the ocean. "Whatever wave you want ... it's yours. You cherry-pick it."

Some other guys pipe in with "Hell yeah." Grace eats it up. And I love that everyone is being cool. Although I hate that Damien comes off as her protector. You'd think he owned the Pacific. I have no problem helping Mr. Parker keep guys like him away from Grace. In fact, I'd say it was in everyone's best interest. I'm starting to see the good side of making a deal with Mr. Parker. Grace needs someone to field guys for her.

––––––––

After driving around aimlessly for about an hour after dinner, I finally pull into an empty parking lot by Black's Beach. Between the stress of watching out for Grace and wondering what I can do to help Little Hien, I'm scrambled.

Esmerelda's engine cuts out with a rattle and a hum when I shut her down. I jump out of the cab and get set up in the bed of the truck. I wad a beach towel into a ball, and lie back on it. There are hundreds of stars out tonight. Twinkling. Sometimes I come out here and talk to PoPo, Ma's *Papi*, but tonight I need to talk to someone I haven't talked to in a long time. Jorge.

It never felt weird talking to PoPo. But talking to somebody your age in Heaven? The ache starts in my throat and spreads all the way down to my chest, where it lies heavy, mixed with the weight of guilt and the sting of reality.

C'mon, now. Man up. Just do it.

I gaze up and find the Milky Way. Then find Sagittarius. The archer. A warrior. The best kind of constellation to find Jorge peeking through. Sometimes, I imagine the sounds of bullets popping off like a truck backfiring in some open-air market in Mexico. And Jorge standing there next to some little kid. Then he grabs the kid and throws him to the ground out of the spray of bullets. And when the shots stop firing the kid is safe and his mom runs to him and Jorge to thank him for her son's life. But it's too late, because Jorge's not there anymore. I don't know how it went down, but I know Jorge's heart. And if there was a chance to save someone else, Jorge would have died doing it. That's the only thing I can hold on to when reality spins out of control.

I stare at the brightest star, a lump in my throat. I croak out, "Hey man. You got time to talk tonight?"

Then I wait. The only noise is cars in the distance zipping down the highway and ocean waves rolling gently in.

"Jorge? I'm sorry, man. I'm so sorry. I couldn't even go to your funeral. Didn't find out about things until too late." I shut my eyes for a brief second. Pull it together. Tighten my grip on the towel and try again. "I didn't know things were that bad. I thought you were in the process of trying to make things legal. Didn't know you could get deported when you were trying to figure out how to do it right. I should have hid your family at my house. Should have figured out how to get you a better lawyer."

Mi Dios. A sob escapes me and I shove my fist into my mouth. I don't deserve to cry. I have my cozy life.

Life.

Jorge? He was just getting started. My breathing heaves up and down with the weight of sobs stuffed inside my ribs until it seems like I'll burst. And for a few minutes all I can do is breathe and fight the release of stuffed emotions, ones that give me *fuego* to fight for all the Jorges. For their families. The stars blur, and I swipe at my eyes and pull it all back in.

My words come out broken. "I'll ... make it ... up. I swear." I sit up and rub the towel on my face. "I save up half of every paycheck. Once I figure out where your mom is living, I'm going to mail her half of this summer's pay." It almost hurts to stare straight at that star. Like I can't look Jorge in the eyes. "I know it doesn't fix things. But I know you would have done the same. Taken care of your family."

I sit up and scoot back until I'm leaning against the cab. Then I hold the towel in my lap and sit in silence.

For several minutes. Calming down. Then I look up one last time. "I'm going to spend my life making this right. I'm going to help people, and Little Hien's my first chance at redemption."

nine

Surfing expresses ... a pure
yearning for visceral, physical
contact with the natural world.
—Matt Warshaw, *Maverick's*

I grab hold of the back of a park bench and stretch my calves. Mom is busy stretching her quads. Our weekly run has been good for us. Mom started it the summer I met Ford, when it seemed like we couldn't get along in regards to anything. It was her peace offering, an attempt to help our relationship. And it has helped—some. It's good for us to spend time together when we're not bickering. One of the best things about running with my mom is not talking. We hang out, run down the same trails, and maintain our own thoughts and differences without feeling the need to get into a verbal sparring session.

A middle-aged man running past pulls a double take, his

eyes lingering on Mom's chest for a split second. Her blond hair, normally layered around her face, is pulled back in a ponytail and, between her muscles and her tan, she looks pretty hot, even if she is mom to a teenager.

Mom stretches her arms behind her, unconsciously pushing her chest out; an old man walking past slows his turtle pace.

"Have you been checking out the Ivy Leagues? Organizing applications?"

I lie, only because the truth would cause a huge argument. In her world, there are no colleges but Ivy League. "Yep."

Mom grins. "Good."

This is my in. "Hey mom, there's a bonfire at the beach next weekend, complete with guitars and off-key singing. Ford's offered to take me, watch out for me. Is it all right if I go?"

I can see the wheels turning in her head. She scrunches up her face, which gives way to a slight frown. "He's a good friend, isn't he?"

I touch my toes. "Yes."

She bends down, stretching all the way to her toes, and then looks over at me. "Make sure that's the way it stays. Just friends. He seems like a good kid, but you don't need a guy distracting you from academics."

"Yes, Mom."

She flips right-side-up and stretches toward the sky. "Good girl. A distraction of the romantic sort of any kind is the last thing you need. Wait until you're attending an Ivy to find the right guy. So you really want to go to this party?"

An unintentional whine escapes. "I totally want to go, and Ford's going to make sure everything's above board."

Mom stops stretching to consider my argument. "Well, you've been working hard at your summer studies, *and* if Ford's going to watch out for you and you're just going together as friends…"

"Just friends. I promise." I beg with my entire body: eyebrows raised, lips parted, hands clasped, down on one knee. Forget pride. Think party.

"I think we can make that happen. I'll talk it over with your father. I don't see him saying no. He's very proud of your class ranking, and it *is* summertime."

I give her a quick hug. "Thanks, Mom. It's way cool of you."

She hugs me back. "Well, I'm not always a party pooper. Is there anything you want to talk about?"

Of course, there's a ton to talk about. Namely, what happened to me three days ago. But she'll talk with me about things until I have no emotional energy left. She'll point out all the ways I set him off. She'll question how much of my side of the story is true. How violent was he, really? She'll go through all the arguments for needing a father figure. Then she'll end the conversation, because the obvious decision after all the "logical" arguments is to stay.

I suck in my breath and hold it a second. What's the point? She'll throw out her made-up statistics regarding what's worse: having a dad who loses his temper sometimes or having no dad at all.

So as a matter of fact, I don't want to discuss it. I'd rather savor my permission to attend the bonfire. "Nah. Let's hit the trail."

————

Six weeks to go until the competition. I attach my leash to my left ankle and wade into the water. Cold water laps against my legs and creeps in through my suit.

"Grrr!"

Ford laughs and splashes behind me, his board jostling against his body as he catches up to me. I continue wading out, ensuring he has to match my pace. Today I'm supposed to pretend I'm competing. I splash onward, determined to act like a badass even if that's the furthest thing from the truth. Because if I don't "fake it until I make it," then all my dreams and hard work might as well be litter floating out on a riptide.

The water hits my thighs and I hop on the board and paddle out, again taking the lead. I don't know if Ford's buying what I'm selling, but that doesn't matter anyway. What does matter is that I deliver. It means everything. Even though the real competition is weeks away, it doesn't stop the nervous jitters running through me.

A wave pitches forward and, as it's about to crash, I duck dive—and it freakin' works! First time I've ever had the strength to push my board down under a wave. I'm stoked I'm already seeing improvements after a week.

The wave passes; I paddle over toward the lineup to wait with the usual crew. I wave at Buzzy and Damien.

Ford joins the lineup about five feet over to my right. "Nice moves getting out here, Parker. You look like a pro."

A wave passes through and we drop down on our boards, turn around, and paddle. It's too late to catch the wave and if we aren't careful, we'll be sucked into it and pulled toward the shore.

Some surfer who dropped in on the wave near me yells, "Out of my way, femme."

Adrenaline pumping, I paddle left fast. If you get run over because you're in someone's wave, not only does it hurt but everyone thinks you're a shubie—a poser, a fake.

Once out of the way, I turn around to see three surfers on the same wave.

Ford sits tall on his board. "I hate party waves."

"Me too."

He pops back down. "Incoming. Paddle, Grace! Let's catch this one together!"

I drop down on my board and look behind me to gauge the wave. It hasn't broken yet. I paddle like there's no tomorrow. The wave begins to suck me and my board up to the top. I lean my weight forward and paddle harder. The board drops down to the trough of the wave and pulls out in front. I pop up and look to my left, stoked about my start.

Ford's standing up too, with matted, wet hair stuck to the side of his face.

I focus and pull a hard bottom turn to the right and veer up the midline face of the wave. The momentum of the wave pulls me forward, bleeding speed. At the top of the wave I pull my very first floater, riding across it. Just as quickly, I pop back down to the bottom, picking up more speed as I land back in the flat zone. Keeping my head facing the line, I repeat the maneuver and begin a short series of floaters, pumping my board up and down from the top of the wave to the midsection, creating my own Grace Parker ocean roller coaster. I love the feeling of the wave below me, propelling me forward. That need to pay close attention to it and constantly adjust for an optimal ride.

I carve hard one last time and then bail as the wave fizzles.

Cheers erupt from a few fellow surfers followed by a barrage of remarks.

Damien paddles over and gives me a hug. "Great job, babe. You really nailed it."

Ford says, "Lay off it, horndog."

Damien says, "Yeah, brah. Who do you think taught her that?"

Ford parks his board next to mine, still frowning about Damien. "That must have been some ride. What'd you pull?"

Annoyed by his over-protectiveness, I keep it minimal. "A floater."

Damien keeps his board next to mine. Knowing it's totally going to piss Ford off, I ask Damien, "Can we work on airs again?"

ten

Coco Nogales is a surfer from Mexico City, who sold gum as a homeless kid until he heard of Puerto Escondido. He moved there after saving up money for seven months to buy a bus ticket. Now he's a world-class surfer.
—according to *The Wave* by Susan Casey

I'm stoked. Today I'm surprising Grace—taking her to a skate park. She's gonna flip. Most surfers skateboard, but Grace has never tried it. I think it's fear. But I'm going to teach her how to surf on concrete and reinforce some skills she needs for a 360. It's a great way to have fun and to get her away from chumps like Damien for an afternoon. I need to make up for screwing up the other day at the beach. It was obvious I kind of pissed Grace off when I popped off at Damien.

As I drive through a part of town Grace has probably never seen, a big pang hits me in the gut. This is—was—

Jorge's hood. He's the reason I even feel comfortable coming here. I pull into Rick D's Skate Park.

Grace squeaks, "Skateboarding?"

"Longboarding, Parker, longboarding," I say. "It's a great way to work on your footwork, like cross-stepping. And then we'll work on some footwork to help you with the elusive 360."

"Falling onto water has a lot less consequences than onto concrete." She twists her hands around, eyeing the Dervish, a freaking awesome longboard skateboard.

Bam. I cock my head at her and enjoy giving her the Look. The mom look. Might be the only time I get to use it. "Are you turning chicken?"

She flaps her arms and says, "Bawk."

I laugh. "At least you'll admit it. Helmets, pads, and Kevlar gloves will help protect you from getting all scraped up."

She folds her arms across her chest. "What about broken bones?" Then she glances around. "Or bullets?"

The bullets comment irritates me. "This place is all good during the day. Just don't hang around here at night." Still, a little uneasy, I glance around just in case. Yeah, that happens every now and then in this neighborhood. But not at the skate park. And not in the daytime. I brush those concerns off with a wave of the hand. "We're not riding a half-pipe or ramps, just a course with a gentle slope. It's as beginner as it gets. Besides, you forget how good your balance is."

She frowns. "I don't have the gear."

She's grasping at straws now. "I bought a board here

last summer. The guy who works here said he'd hook us up with gear for you to borrow."

Ten minutes later, I'm watching Grace adjust the strap to her helmet, which is lopsided. I reach over. "Dude. Let me help." She lifts her chin and looks at me, grateful. I'm enjoying the moment. Tightening the strap, touching her just below her delicate jawline. Cheesy, yes. But true. All the way.

I pass her the gloves.

She says, "I'm about to pee my pants."

I laugh. "No worries. I'll say you're with someone else."

She pushes me. My skin warms where her hand should still be.

She says, "When'd you learn how to do this?"

I laugh. "Every little boy skateboards. At least the cool ones do. But Jorge got me into the tricks and stuff."

She gives me a sad look. That's the one look I don't want. I ignore it. I'll have my day. Someday. In court. When I'm on the side of folks like Jorge. He could have been the next Coco Nogales. But Jorge's six feet under and Grace's pity looks don't change shit. Her naive and flippant sympathy irritate me. Somebody like her dad should have handled Jorge's case. But his firm only takes so many pro bono cases. The whole deal sucks. Period.

I harden myself. Shrug her off. "I usually practice in the afternoons, after you go home."

"What's up with being so secretive?" she asks.

"I don't have to tell you everything. I've skateboarded forever. It's time to branch out—hence, longboarding. I have my secrets." I hop on my Dervish and carve big arcs on the sidewalk. I walk up and down the Dervish, cross-stepping like it's a surfboard.

Grace fiddles with the frayed edge of a pair of shorts. "Show off."

I keep it up. "Jealous."

She shrugs. "Maybe."

I stop by running my board into the grass and flip off it into the air.

Grace screeches, "What the heck? You could break your neck."

I cup my hands over my mouth and bass before playfully mocking Grace. "What the heck? I could break my neck," followed by rap-sounding noises.

She pushes into me with her side. "Quit it. I'm serious."

I bass some more, beatbox, and rap, "Qu-qu-qu-quit it. Qu-qu-qu-quit it. The little lady's scared I'll bit it." I quit and tug at my chinstrap.

"I don't suggest you pursue a career as a rapper, and you might want to work on the whole staying-in-the-same-verb-tense thing."

"Aw, c'mon, girl. You know I'm irresistible."

"Whatev. No more flipping in the air off moving objects. It freaks me out."

I shrug. "Let's start you off as basic as it gets—carving. It's all in the hips. Pretend you're carving on the water and that's pretty much it."

She makes a point of eyeing the board and then the concrete.

"Check it. I'll walk next to you while you get started.

You can even hold on to me for balance. We'll take it super slow and let you feel the rhythm." I stand in front of her, the board at our feet between us, holding my hands out.

She grabs hold of my hands. Her board rolls back and forth a little. She tightens her grip.

I smile. "See, no *problemas*. Now I'll walk forward and when you feel comfortable, sway your hips back and forth, keeping your feet in the same position they would be on your surfboard. It's easy. Promise."

I walk sideways, facing Grace. She's tense, I hold on to her and smile. A few feet later, she relaxes a bit.

"That's it. Loosen up. Try turning your hips. I'll stay with you."

She nods. She's in the zone. She turns her hips and a smile creeps across her face.

She whispers, "It's like surfing concrete."

I'm not even sure she knows she said anything out loud. Her face is lit up like a kid at Christmas. She lets go of my hands and weaves back and forth, gliding on the sidewalk.

This is one of the few times outside of surfing I've seen her this relaxed. This happy. My day is made.

She carves big arcs. Getting confident. Maybe too much. She tightens her curves and her speed picks up. I jog toward her. She's headed straight for a patch of grass. Shit. She didn't give me a chance to teach her how to—she nails the grass and hops off the board. Whew.

I say, "Whaddya think?"

She lies down on a patch of green. "I think this is amazing."

I join her. "You ready to learn how to cross-step?"

She turns to face me. "You know it."

I roll to my side and face her. "Think we can include this in our training regimen?"

She lights up from the inside out. "Heck yeah. This is total clutch."

I raise my hand for a high five. She meets me midair. We connect for the slightest moment. I curl my fingers around hers for a moment before letting go. Holding hands with Grace is like playing with fire, and I'm not much on getting burned.

eleven

Reality has become so intolerable,
she said, so bleak, that all I can paint
now are the colors of my dreams.
—Azar Nafisi, *Reading Lolita in Tehran*

By the time Saturday night arrives, I'm stoked about attending my first bonfire.

Mom and Dad decide to enjoy dinner and a night out at the movies. Things have been okay since the episode last week. Whatever it was, Dad's seemed to get things out of his system, for a while at least. I'm not naive enough to believe things are different. He's making the effort to be on his best behavior again. I take what I can get, and Mom seems happy they're getting along for the moment.

After stressing out over which outfit to wear, I end up choosing a light green sundress with an empire waist. I put it on, and then I look in the mirror and play around with my hair. Hold it in different pigtails. Ten minutes later, I have two loose French braids parted down the middle and flowing back into a messy bun. It looks awesome. Messy. Cute. Sexy.

I put on lip gloss and mascara. Then I head for the living room and wait for Ford to pick me up. It's funny, but I know the only person standing between me and a no-strings-attached night is Ford. The one all my strings are attached to. I can't risk them getting snipped. He's not the one for a flirty, fun night. He's too important for that. But he's the one picking me up.

He knocks on the door at a minute past eight.

I walk calmly to the door and swing it open with a huge grin.

Ford makes no pretense he isn't drinking me in with his eyes and ends up focusing on my face. "Dang, *Mamacita*."

I say, "You ready?"

He looks into the house. "Do I need to check in with your parents or anything?"

I shake my head no. "They're getting ready to go on a date."

And hello, right on cue, Dad walks into the room, wearing an immaculate linen suit. He defies the laws of wrinkles.

I say, "Hey Daddy. We were just about to head out."

Dad strides across toward us. He shakes Ford's hand and his voice booms, "So you're taking Grace to a bonfire tonight."

Ford's smile seems a little strained as my dad keeps shaking his hand. "Yes sir."

Dad claps his other hand on top of Ford's and all motion

stops before the handshake ends. "I'm counting on you to take good care of my baby girl."

Ford stands like a soldier at attention. "Yes sir. You can count on me."

"That's the idea. You heard about Mierl's latest case? I'm telling you, those are some sharp guys. Well, enough office talk. You two have fun."

Ford says, "Yes sir."

I tug onto Ford and we walk out to Esmerelda. Man, Dad laid it on thick tonight. Poor Ford all but saluted him.

Who cares? We're free and I feel super cute in my dress. I half skip to his truck.

"Who are you trying to impress?" Ford asks.

"Nobody in particular. How about guys in general?" I laugh softly. Is the world spinning faster tonight? Everything is dizzyingly beautiful. Tonight is happy. I'm happy.

"You sure you don't want to go get a sweater or something...so you can cover up?" Ford mutters as he opens the passenger-side door and I walk down our front porch steps.

I ignore the Grampa remark and scoot in. Ford shoves the passenger door closed. He struts to the driver's seat and starts the engine. U2 is playing on the radio. They're one of my faves.

"Sweet." I don't know if it's the excitement of my first real beach party or the fact that I feel like Rapunzel freed from her tower, but I'm feeling a bit reckless. I'm sick of trying so hard to color in the lines. To say the right thing. To walk the tightrope across the Niagara Falls that is my home.

And then there's this tension, always beneath the surface

when I'm around Ford. This attraction I have to keep at bay. I try to pretend like tonight is normal and nothing between us will ever change. But somewhere deep down, I worry it will. Relationships are like the ocean; always there, but the conditions never stay the same. Even some of the sweetest surf spots in the world have crappy days.

Ford pulls up into the beach parking lot and leaves Esmerelda running. "Okay, Parker. Here's the lowdown. The usual crew will be there. Alcohol will be involved. If someone hands you punch, don't drink it. If you drink anything, make sure it comes out of a can you open."

I roll my eyes. "Okay, big brother. I'm not the village idiot."

"Hey, you usually don't come to this kind of stuff. I want to make sure you're okay. And, in spite of your *I'm a big girl* attitude, if anyone bothers you, let me know and I'll take care of him. All right?"

Impatient, I bounce on the seat like a little kid. "Oh, okay. I'll call you if someone tries to feel me up. Now let's go."

I start to push my shoulder into the passenger door.

He grins. "Nope. Tonight, milady, I'll take care of that!" He hops out, runs around the truck, and opens my door. He tumbles an imaginary top hat off his head and bows.

Once more, I laugh. It feels good. A slight spark ignites, the kind that couldn't flourish at home. Not enough oxygen. But I remind myself tonight is not the night for sparks to fly. Tamp it down, tamp it down.

The bonfire blazes, little sparks getting caught up in the wind and eventually blowing out in one final glow. One of the local crew strums a guitar, adding a melodic quality to this bohemian shindig.

"Parker? Let's snag these lawn chairs."

I turn around and the fire's reflection shines on his black hair. He's sitting in a ratty old lawn chair and gesturing to a red-striped one next to him. I join him and stare at the fire, enjoying the general chaos. People all over the place are in various stages of flirting, hooking up, getting drunk, dancing, or breaking up. Another in-my-face reason not to get together with Ford. And then there's my promise to Mom. Besides, high school relationships don't last. There's an endless supply of drama to watch safely from my vantage point. I prop my feet up on the edge of Ford's chair and inhale everything from the salty ocean air to smoke from the fire to an occasional whiff of beer as folks pass by.

Ford puts his hand on my foot. I tense up, unsure about what to do. That small amount of real estate on my ankle is enough to undo all my resolves.

My mouth's as dry as cotton balls. "I'm thirsty."

He starts to get up.

"No worries. I got it." I escape, scurrying off toward the coolers, leaving him with an empty lawn chair.

I pass Damien. He checks me out in such an obvious way, I'd normally blow him off, but I'm flipping out and he's been giving me rides, helping me with moves. I know he's got more depth than Ford would have me believe.

I feel on edge and scrambled.

I stare right back at him and we connect. I take two

steps and he finishes off the distance between us in a few quick strides. He's wearing a Volcom hat and board shorts.

He does the *double head bob I'm cool* move and says, "Come here often?"

I tilt my head and try to look coy. "No. You?"

"Maybe I would if more girls like you came here." He gives a wide grin, his teeth super white in contrast to his dark skin. His dreads are chill and make him look that much hotter.

"Well, maybe I will."

"Damn, girl."

I blush. I didn't mean to come on to him that strong.

He cocks his head at me. "It's all good."

I place my hand on his muscled forearm and croak, "*Yeah*, it is."

He seems amused, his lips curled in a faint smile. His eyes switch focus for a millisecond somewhere behind me.

I turn around to see Ford, who's now two steps away from us with a couple of Gatorades.

Oh man. He's taking this big brother thing way too serious. He's not in charge of me.

Ford says, "Hey, guys. Grace, you said you were thirsty. I brought you a drink."

I say, "Hey, Ford. Thanks." I look back and forth between the guys and watch Ford's usually calm expression tense up.

Damien peers down at Ford, then reaches out and takes the other drink. He says, "Thanks, Brah."

Ford's too stunned to move. "What?"

Damien says, "C'mon girl. Let's dance." He takes a

sip of the Gatorade and hands it back to Ford. Then he places his hat on me and slowly backs up toward a crowd of people dancing. He motions for me to follow him, and even though I feel like I might be setting something irreversible into motion, I perversely take a few steps, knowing it would be easier to lose someone who isn't my lifeblood—losing Ford would undo me in more ways than I could count.

Confused and anxious, I set my drink on a nearby cooler.

Ford's face has turned panicky. "I promised your folks I'd take care of you."

Damien laughs. "It's all good. We're not running off anywhere secret, Brah. We're dancing." Then he points. "Right over there, in plain sight."

Ford's eyes turn into slits. I can tell he's annoyed by the way he works his jaw. He needs to realize he's not on the clock right now. I wish Dad hadn't said anything to him—he took that whole "take care of my baby girl" speech way too seriously.

I make an uncomfortable face at him and follow Damien, to the background of Bob Marley and the Wailers. This is out of control. Ford's gonna be pissed. But this is a bonfire. It's fun. Flirty. No strings attached. This is my one night to party. Things have been crazy at home—I just want one night with nothing on the line. Is that too much to ask?

Damien's got the moves. His dancing makes me self-conscious. I'm not even close to his league. He dances toward me, hips swaying to the beat. He closes in on me and all of a sudden what was a couple of feet of space between us is now a couple of inches. The heat between us is palpable as we move in unison.

What was intended to be a quick dance turns into more songs than I can keep track of. Damien's a freaking awesome dancer. He moves to the beat, kicking in an extra one every now and then with a shake of his chest. It makes me laugh and want to dance until the sun comes up and dissolves the magic that flourishes in the night. Then he spreads his arms out wide, shaking his hips and bobbing his knees at the same time. I shake my way in closer. And the best thing about Damien? He never settles down with anyone. I feel like Cinderella at the ball, but I welcome the safe pumpkin ending, because glass slippers belong in fairy tales.

If it weren't for the few glances I keep stealing at Ford because of the ridiculous amount of guilt gnawing at me, I'd be having a lot more fun. I feel like such a jerk. But Ford seems okay now. He went from sitting by himself in a lawn chair to picking up a guitar and playing with a couple of guys. Girls are already headed his way.

I can't stand it. I need to go over and make sure everything's good between us.

The song fades out, and before Damien's hands on my hips make me forget my need to check in on things with Ford, I pull away—barely.

"I need to go check on something. Maybe I can catch another dance in a few songs?"

"Catch ya later, babe." Then he shrugs, like no biggie. His head's already moving in rhythm with the new song, dreads swaying to a new beat.

I walk over to Ford, winding my way through a few groups of people. He looks so cute, playing guitar. I get a big goofy grin on my face and say, "How's it going?"

Ford stops strumming for a millisecond and then starts back up again. He says, "Oh, it's cool. Yeah, things are real cool."

Feeling somewhat disappointed, although I'm not sure why, I say, "Good. I'm glad you're having a good time."

What is up with us, using the words "cool" and "good"? Hello? We have a plethora of options to choose from, thanks to the SAT.

Feeling awkward because Ford doesn't say a word, I say, "Sweet. Well, I'll find you later."

I turn around and head back toward Damien, feeling a little distant and awkward after talking to Ford. More than anything, I feel kind of lonely. Damien's dreadlocks swaying above the rest of the crowd catch my eye. We connect once again and he nods and waves for me to come back over and dance. It perks me up a little. I strut over to him, realizing that in my absence the Betties have begun flocking. Instead of the two of us dancing, I'll be one of a group of girls gathered around him. He laughs, and I'm not sure if it's because of all the girls or because he loves dancing so much.

So much for flirting, so much for feeling special. I retreat and make my way back over to Ford. My stomach sinks. He's not alone anymore.

Awesome. Anna, one of the ho-bags of the century, is writing something on his hand and leaning into him all seductive. Then she walks off, in search of someone else to flirt with.

I bristle on the inside but wear an *I couldn't care less* look. "Hey, Ford. Having fun?"

"Yeah, I am. As a matter of fact, that hot mama gave me her number."

I snort. She'd give anybody that, and a lot more. "Cool."

Ford reaches over and takes Damien's hat off my head. "What's up with wearing a brodaddy hat?"

"Nothing." I swipe at it, but he holds it away from me.

"Then I guess you won't mind if I do this." He places it on the head of a passing drunk girl. "It's really not your style."

"Yeah, well, maybe not."

He says, "What's the problem?"

Inwardly fuming, I check my watch. "Nothing. I don't know. I've gotta be home soon."

"Oh yeah," Ford says, "I forgot you turn into a pumpkin at midnight."

We walk back to the truck in awkward silence, with me biting off the urge to correct him on the fact that the carriage turns into a pumpkin and the coachman turns into a rat. When we reach Esmerelda, Ford unlocks the door and walks around to his side. No gallantries this time. I guess it's up to me to rip the door open. I do, and end up flinging myself into the car parked next to us.

Ford plays it off, saying, "Oh sorry. I forgot. My bad."

I nod and say, "No big deal."

This is so stupid. Normally we'd laugh if something like this happened, and then we'd hop in his truck and blast out of here before someone griped about their precious paint job. I stare at the moon for a while, trying not to be the one who breaks the silence. But the thought of Ford and Anna makes me cringe.

I say, "So you got Anna's number."

Ford drums on the steering wheel. "Yep. She's pretty cute too. I might give her a call."

That shreds my last semblance of patience. I completely make something up. "I don't know. I heard she's in a love triangle or something." Anna is always playing multiple guys; it can't be too far from the truth. Only thing is, I don't know who the current tools are.

"I don't know," Ford says. "I might call her anyway. She's not too into it if she's giving me her number. Besides, I like squares."

"You did not just say that."

"Did she say anything to you about me?"

I would have clawed her face. "Don't get all cocky. It's unattractive."

"I can't help it if the ladies like me. Some people have good taste."

It's like he can't leave it alone. I roll my eyes and look out the window.

twelve

*torta: in Mexico, a sandwich served
on white crusty bread (a bolillo)
and usually centered around a meat*

After the Bonfire from Hell gone wrong, I didn't even need my alarm this morning. I'm ready to get to work. To take my mind far away from the beach and douche bag Damien and whether or not that tool will ruin my future career. To be with people who are who they are. To have fun with Brianna and Hop.

Ma set out a bag of *tortas* to share at the office. Score.

After grabbing Teresa a chai tea at Lola's Coffee, I pull into the parking garage fifteen minutes early. That's how pathetic my summer has become. Or maybe how crazy guarding Grace has driven me.

I take the stairs and notice again how posh everything in this building is: the glass staircase, the stone walls, the fountains, the grass planters everywhere. The modern way of saying, "Do business with us. We're hip, calm, successful."

I think about the office Jorge spent hours and hours waiting in. The one with drab walls, long lines of plastic chairs, and more people than seats. The pro bono lawyer who helped illegal immigrants wade through paperwork. Go through the right channels. The dude did his best. But that wasn't good enough. He didn't have the resources of a firm with rich clients. He didn't have a lot. The one thing he had was a good heart.

I didn't even get to say good-bye. I should have taken Jorge in—should have let him hide out at my house. But I didn't. I didn't know. And then he got caught in the crossfire between local police and drug runners. One of the big reasons his family left a country they loved was safety and opportunity. That's why I'm going pro bono. Those are the peeps I'm going to help. For-real help. I'll earn my chops with a big firm, then break off and do my thing.

I open the door to the office. Teresa looks up. I smile. "Morning, *Mamacita*." She does the Look. "What is it with you women and the Look?" I ask. "I swear I'm on my best behavior." Her eyebrows rise higher. Didn't know that was possible. I lay on a thick accent to mess with her. "Watch out, they might get stuck." She starts to protest. I slide her tea from Lola's over. "Chai tea. *Para ti*."

She smiles. "*Gracias*."

I nod. "*De nada*."

Then I sit in my usual spot. Brianna will show up any minute. Hop will roll in last with his latest crazy bus story.

The door opens and Brianna blazes in with extensions, hundreds of tiny new braids, all over her head. She's wearing another sexy office outfit. White slacks that show off curvy hips. A dark brown top that hugs full curves. Even her shoes are cute. I let loose a quiet whistle.

Instead of giving me the Look, she says, "You too."

I pull my shirt away from my chest like I'm burning up. "Well, I am wearing clean clothes. And I did iron them this morning."

She laughs and sits down next to me. "Ford, you're a funny guy."

"What's the difference between fun and fungi?"

She leans in. "I don't know. What?"

"One gets you ladies. The other gets you eaten."

She pushes my arm. "That was bad."

Grace's little act last night still burns me. The royal flush was a royal pain. I flash Brianna a wicked grin and alternate flexing my pecs. "I'm a bad boy."

She leans down and grabs the bag of *tortas* Ma made for the office. "What did we bring today?"

Hop walks in as I say, "*Tortas*."

He says, "Dude. My fave. Can I have one? Breakfast was more of a wish than a reality this morning. I was running late."

Brianna and I eye each other and shake our heads in disbelief. I say, "You? Late? Never."

She dangles the sack in the air.

Hop reaches for it. Brianna drops it in my lap and blocks me with her body. Her legs feel good pressed against mine.

Hop says, "C'mon. Where's the hope for Hop?" Then he says, "Fine. I'll tell jokes until you relent."

Brianna turns around and grabs the bag out of my lap, so fast that her boobs brush my biceps. And while she's handing over a couple of *tortas*, I enjoy the warm feeling of Brianna on my arm.

Teresa takes a sip of tea before saying, "This is a law office. And some mornings the three of you are one clown short of a circus."

We all pause midair. Teresa made a joke. A funny one.

Hop finishes his bite of *torta*. "You've been holding out on us."

She deadpans, "Someone has to keep you hopping, Hop."

We all crack up.

She shoos us down the hall. "Go to Jada. She might have something new for you this morning."

We race down the hallway freaking out about the possibility of moving beyond stamping, sorting, and labeling.

———

Jada greets us with a grunt as she struggles to move a box twice her size.

Hop and I rush over to help her. I say, "Where would you like it?"

Jada steps away and rubs at her wrists. "In the corner ... I'm expecting to receive quite a load regarding the Thompson case today."

"Dang. This *is* heavy." I heft it over there. Then I turn around. "Next time feel free to wait for me or Hop to get here."

She gives a terse grin. "How fast are you on the freeway? I have a doc that needs to be delivered within the hour."

I think about Esmerelda breaking down and I shrug, embarrassed. "Um, my truck isn't always reliable. I wouldn't want to miss the deadline 'cause I'm on the side of the road."

Hop says, "Who needs a license when the mass transportation options are so alluring?"

Brianna says, "We can take my car, if Ford will drive for me. I don't do downtown traffic unless I'm desperate."

Jada says, "Deal. Hop, you're with me for the next hour. I'm going to show you how to transcribe affidavits."

Ugh. I'm driving around in a car and Hop gets to learn the cool stuff.

Hop doesn't say a word, which in itself is way louder than if he had said something. And the grin on his face is more than enough.

Jada looks between the three of us and blows out some air. "Oh, fine. I'll show you two when you get back, unless there's some other little thing you'd like to learn."

"What's the paperwork a person would file to get legal status?" Crap. That flew out of my mouth a little too fast.

Jada turns her head to the side and gets a worried look on her face. "Is this for you, hon?"

I shake my head no emphatically. "Nah. It's for a friend."

Brianna and Jada exchange a look.

"Seriously. It's this guy I play poker with … right, Hop?"

"Yeah," Hop whispers.

We both eye Jada and wait. She says, "Let me think about the best info to get you. But my gut feeling is there's not much that can be done."

Anger boils up. I shove it back down, knowing Jada's just telling it straight. But that doesn't make it any easier to swallow. "Okay. Let me know if you come up with anything."

Jada's face softens. "I will." Then she grabs a manila envelope off the counter and hands it to me. "Address is on the cover." She checks her watch. "You got fifty-five minutes."

Brianna's little car is tight quarters. My knees are inches from my ears.

Brianna asks, "So who is this guy you're wanting to help?"

I focus on the road. "One of Hop's buddies."

Out of the corner of my eye, I see her playing with her bracelet. She says, "That's really cool, but why doesn't your friend just get a lawyer?"

"Money. Some folks have it. Some don't." I can hear that tension in my voice, but I can't get rid of it. I speed up, switch lanes, and pass a couple of cars. It's dumb that it makes me feel better. I press down on the pedal and pass another few cars.

Brianna holds the help-me-God handle. "I think we'll get there on time, Ford."

I let up on the accelerator. "Sorry. If we get there late, my ass is grass."

"This legal-status stuff seems pretty personal when it's for someone you just met."

I shrug.

She says, "You wanna talk about it?"

I don't want to talk about what happened to Jorge. "Maybe later."

"Okaaaaay. Change of subject." Then she adds, "You know what, Ford? I've always wanted to surf. But I've been too nervous to try. I haven't hung out with surfers before you."

"I could teach you," I say, thankful for the change of subject. "It's pretty easy. I've heard I'm a decent coach."

Brianna squeals and plays with her seat belt. "All right! What about this afternoon?"

She's so excited and cute. I think about it. It was really cool for her not to push me. I hesitate and then say, "Sure. Today's great. I'll meet you at Encinitas. It's a bit shifty on the break, but it's a decent place to learn. It's a sand bottom and we'll stay on the inside."

She laughs. "I love surf lingo."

———

An hour and a half after we get off work, I meet Brianna in the parking lot at Encinitas. She steps out of her car in a spicy bikini. It's white and tiny and shows off all her curves. And while it's mighty fine to look at, clearly she's never surfed. That sucker will get washed right off of her. And she'll freeze. She's so excited she's practically bouncing over to me.

I clear my throat. "That's a great swimsuit."

"Thanks."

Then I grab a wetsuit out of the truck and pull it over my legs. "Did you bring anything to wear over it?"

She wrinkles her nose. "No. I have a long-sleeve shirt—will that work?"

Oh man. She makes clueless so sexy. Never would have thought that possible before now. "Have you ever been swimming at the beach before?"

She shrugs. "The water's too cold. But I figured, you know, with the excitement of surfing, maybe I could deal."

I grin. "No way."

Her face falls.

I quit pulling my wetsuit on, leaving it hanging around my waist. "And that's why you have me. I kind of figured you might need one. I brought an old wetsuit for you to try. It might be a little big, but it'll be way better than nothing. Trust me."

She does a little dance; her braids bounce around her face. "I knew you would be the perfect coach. You're awesome and we haven't even gotten in the water yet."

I pass it over to her. I do my best to look the other way

while she wiggles into my old suit. How much can a guy take? Every little glance … I see something jiggle. In the best way possible.

She laughs. "Ford, you're so funny. It's on. You can look now. Besides I need your help. How do you zip this thing up?"

I walk over and step up behind her. I thought the suit might be big on her. And it certainly doesn't fit her like it fits me, but her curves seem to fill it out perfectly. The chest on that suit will never be the same. I reach down to grab the zipper dangling above her rear end. I laugh nervously and carefully grab it without touching her. I listen to the sound as I zip her up. I grab my board and say, "C'mon. Time's a wasting."

She walks next to me, looking like a goddess in my suit. It hugs her curves tightly, making her ankles look delicate.

We claim a spot on the beach near a family of tourists. The kind of mom who'll watch our stuff like a hawk while we're out surfing. I wax the board and comb. Brianna quietly watches, squatting down next to me. A foot of space between us. This is nice. The kind of scenario I used to wish I had with Grace. With her interested in me. Hanging on my every word and action. Showing interest instead of pushing me away.

I give her the rundown. "We'll hang out at the foamies. Let you practice standing up. Get the feel for the waves. I'll be right next to you the whole time. Cool?"

She grins. Her whole face lights up. "Cool!"

"Watch me lie down on the sand and pop up. That's what you're going to want to do on the board. It's one fluid motion." I lie down and pop up in slow motion a couple of times, then I show her real time. "You got it?"

She nods. Then she lies down on the sand and practices a few stand-ups. They look pretty decent.

I say, "Let's do it."

We walk out together. Me carrying the board. When her waist hits the water, she squeals and shivers. I laugh. Same thing Grace does. Must be a girl thing.

We stop where the foamies break. I grab the leash. "Put this on your right ankle."

She extends her right leg up to the surface and rests it on the board, ankle in the air. Her toenail polish is bright red. She has cute toes. She fumbles around with the Velcro.

I grab it and say, "Here. It's kind of tricky." I fix it and I swear she's blushing.

"Okay. So lie down on the board. I'll hold on to it for you and I'll push you forward into a wave. Then when you feel comfortable, stand up."

She grabs the rails of my board and scoots onto it, a bit wobbly and too far up.

"Scoot back a little. Your balance will be off."

She scoots back and her rear end hits my arm as she gets settled into a better spot. My forearm. Across her butt. A modern-day miracle.

I stabilize the board. "How does it feel?"

"I'm ready." She squints up at me, flashing a gorgeous smile. I smile back, clueless of what to say next.

A split second later, a small wave comes at us. I push her forward and say, "Paddle!"

The wave sweeps her up and even though she doesn't really paddle, she's riding the surfboard. Lying down for a ride that carries her all the way to ankle-deep water. Then she gets up and walks back to me, pushing the board with her hand. Her face is glowing with excitement.

I laugh. So what. She didn't stand up, but she had fun. That's what it's all about.

After about twenty tries, Brianna stands up, and that's when it's time to call it quits. We walk toward the shore. She looks exhausted, but also like she's on that adrenaline high.

The family is gone but our stuff's still around. I grab the bag and toss the wax and the comb into it. Then I stick the board under my arm and we walk back to the parking lot.

Buzzy and Damien drive up, music blaring, and park right by us. Shit. What are the odds? This isn't their usual beach. They get out of Damien's Jeep, a big grin on their faces. Then Damien opens up the passenger door behind him.

Out pops Grace. Double shit.

And Brianna is of course jiggling out of my wetsuit.

Buzz and Damien are both checking Brianna out while she's bent down tugging the wetsuit over her feet. Buzzy gives me a thumbs-up and Damien nods at me like *right on*. I roll my eyes. Grace's arms are folded tightly across her chest, but she has an *I couldn't care less* look on her face.

Brianna stands up and shivers. Goose bumps ripple across

her skin. Then she grabs her towel and wraps up in it. I wish there were more of it, to cover her body better.

Buzzy says, "Hey. You new in town?"

Brianna laughs. "No. Ford was just teaching me how to surf."

Damien leans against his Jeep. "Oh yeah. Our buddy Ford. He's a great teacher." Then he walks around to Brianna and extends his hand. "I'm Damien."

She says, "Brianna."

Buzzy says, "*Nice* to meet you." He all but wolf-whistled in that statement.

Brianna shoots him a wicked grin. "But I didn't meet you."

He blushes. "I'm Buzzy."

She reaches out her hand. "Nice to meet you."

And for the first time in my life, I watch Buzzy's ears turn bright red. Wow. Brianna really does have an effect on guys.

She glances at Grace, who hasn't moved. "Hi. I'm Brianna. And you are?"

Stare-down central. "Grace."

Without any further acknowledgement, Brianna turns back to me. "Thanks for the surf lesson. Maybe we can do it again sometime."

I nod. Awkward, saying good-bye in front of these two goobs and Grace.

"Well. I guess I'll see you Wednesday," she adds. Then she gets in her car, maneuvering between Buzzy and Damien who may as well be puppies with their tails wagging and their tongues hanging out.

Before she drives off, Brianna rolls down the window and holds out a piece of paper. "Here, Ford. I had a lot of fun."

I take it. "Yeah. Me too."

She says, "Well, bye."

"Bye."

She drives off and the four of us stand around stupidly, watching her car disappear from the parking lot. Me holding a small piece of paper with her phone number. In front of Grace. And confused as to why I should be hiding the smile that's trying to take over my face.

thirteen

*Man is a knot into which
relationships are tied.*
—Antoine de Saint-Exupéry

Saturday night keeps running through my mind like a CD that skips. I made such a mess of things flirting with Damien. But what did Ford expect? We're not together and I promised my mom nothing would happen between me and Ford. And he was totally anal about his chaperone role. He didn't even call Sunday to see if I wanted to surf after church. What was up with that? And then there was that girl wearing his old wetsuit at Encinitas yesterday. Grrr.

By dinnertime, I'm mentally and emotionally exhausted and my stomach is growling; untouched college applications (printed out by Mom's administrative assistant) wait.

"Grace, dinner's ready."

"Coming, Mom."

The mounds of college mailers and info packets over-whelm me. It's summertime. I shouldn't have to deal with junk until school starts. I wonder whether or not I'll be able to keep my class rank. The UCSD surf team has high academic standards—being valedictorian on top of being a kick-butt surfer girl might be the deciding factor.

Mom singsongs, "Grace, we're waiting."

"I'm really coming now," I holler, hurrying down the hallway like a good little daughter should. "Smells yummy. What'd you make?"

Dad says, "I decided to give it a whirl tonight." He grins and winks conspiratorially. "So it might not be quite as healthy as usual, but what's a little splurge now and then?"

I grin; he's an awesome cook. "Fantastic. I'm starving!"

He leans down and whips a chef hat onto his head. I clap my hands over my mouth and laugh. With a dramatic flair, he lifts the lid off a covered dish and says in a cheesy French accent that he always uses when cooking, "Voila! What we 'ave here eez a lovely steamed asparagus topped with a hollandaise sauce. You can zee for yourself zee beau-tiful tossed salad. And"—he puts a hand to his mouth and kisses it like the dramatic cooks in the movies—"for zee main course? We have a broiled wild-caught salmon topped with somezing simple—garlic and lemon."

"Yum! I should have raced for zee table!"

We bow our heads and wait for my dad to say the prayer.

———

I'm in the middle of filling out the basics for a college application to Princeton, my dad's alma mater, when my cell buzzes. Technically I shouldn't be taking calls right now, but I check to see who it is—Ford.

I whisper, "Hey. I can't talk long. I'm working on college apps."

"Nice to chat with you too."

I write in *Eco club* on my list of extracurriculars. "What's up?"

"Can we talk Thursday morning?"

I close my eyes. "We're talking now."

"Let's get more specific. This is more of an in-person conversation; I want to see your face. Can I swing by and talk about the other night over breakfast?"

I stop in the middle of writing *Spanish Club Vice President*. Vice president is always the way to go; you get the title but don't have to do anything…unless the president no-shows.

"Parker?"

"Yeah."

"So how about it?"

I swallow. My brain is in a mad scramble to get out of this mess. I'm not sure how to fix things between us, but I never expected Ford to be so up-front.

"Dang," he says. "I mean, it's not like we ended Saturday on the best of notes."

Inhale, exhale. Breakfast at my place won't work. What's

he thinking? I never have anyone over at my house. "Let's go somewhere else."

His voice is quieter than usual. "Yeah, okay."

fourteen

forbear: *to hold oneself back*
from especially with an effort
—www.merriam-webster.com

I'm barely out of my neighborhood when Esmerelda's engine cuts out. Really? This morning? I hit the steering wheel. Then quickly say, "Sorry, girl. I know you do your best."

I pop the hood and stare at the engine.

Forty minutes later I'm back on the road. Sweaty. Greasy. Smelly. Not the way I pictured things today. As I turn the corner to Grace's street, I notice that Esmerelda's added a new screech to her rattle. Great. Just what I need. The only good thing is she didn't break down on a work day.

As I pull into Grace's, I notice she's sitting on her porch like always. She looks pissed.

I get out of Esmerelda and Grace pops up to standing. "What gives?"

"Sorry. Esmerelda gave out on the way here. I've been tinkering around with her engine for the past forty minutes. The good news is she's working for the moment. The bad news is I don't expect it to last. I'll take her by my dad's shop tonight."

"You got a thing against calling me now?"

"I know, sorry." I throw up hands covered in blackish grease. Really? She's so wrapped up in herself she doesn't even notice my pit stains or the grease all over my hands.

Grace takes in a deep breath and blows out her frustration. She's so anal about being on time, it's kind of annoying.

We pick up breakfast tacos and coffee at Lola's, where I use their bathroom to scrub as much grease as possible off my hands and forearms. Grace didn't offer her bathroom, which would have been a totally obvious gesture. She's weird about that kind of stuff.

Our ride to the beach is silent. I haven't figured out what to say, and I guess Grace hasn't either. For the sake of our friendship, my internship, and Grace's future, there's only one thing to do. Patch things up and move forward.

I roll into a parking spot at the empty glider port. This is a day to surf Black's, AKA Torrey Pines State Park among tourists, AKA the nudie beach among concerned moms. My mom? She laughs and calls it *cheap exposure to European-style beaches.* One of my favorite things about Black's? Three-hundred-foot cliffs as a backdrop.

I sit on my tailgate and wait for Grace to quit reorganizing my bag. She's way intense about making more space. When she glances up, her face shining like she won the lottery, I motion her over. That look. The look of excitement. The cute way she scrunches her nose. The first of a million reasons I keep coming back to Grace. That and what Ma calls my savior complex. Always needing to help people. But I still haven't figured out what Grace needs saving from … I just have a feeling. I can't explain it.

"Why don't you snag our breakfast and join me?" I pat a spot on the tailgate next to me.

Grace gets the food. I sip some coffee. She perches on the rusty edge next to me and swings her legs. Mine dangle, still. I grab the bag from her and dig around until I find my order. I nudge the bag over to Grace, but she doesn't reach for her order.

Oh well. I'm starving. I take a massive bite and chew enough to tuck it into the side of my mouth. "So, the way you treated me the other night pretty much stunk."

Grace fiddles with the bottom of her T-shirt, which means she knows I'm right. But I don't see her running to apologize. Typical. And if I don't fix things, then not only will our friendship be screwed up but it'll practically guarantee I can't keep guys away from her, hence breaking the Deal-with-the-Dad. Good-bye girl *and* good-bye future? No thanks.

"I thought we were friends hanging out at a bonfire," I begin. "I get that you don't want to date me. It's cool. For reals. I'm way past it. But you don't have to rub my nose in it. 'Kay? And Damien? Grace, I'm no expert, but you could do way better. Besides, you're training. You don't have time to get involved with someone. It'll just distract you from the comp."

She stops swinging her legs. "Sorry for the stuff I said about Anna. If you want to date her, that's your business."

Really? That's how she's going to play this? Talk about Anna and not even mention Brianna? The other day, Grace's eyes were about to bore a hole in me. She was totally jealous.

I say, "Are you even listening? I don't want to date her, or anyone for that matter. I don't even want to call her. She sounds like she's got her hands full, right?"

Grace laughs. "She's such a ho-bag, and you could do way better."

I take a long look at her, then take another bite of my taco and think about Brianna. Things with her are less complicated. Maybe more fun.

I stare at the bag with the unopened tacos, then switch my gaze to Grace before checking out the waves. "I know."

fifteen

*Failure seldom stops you. What
stops you is the fear of failure.*
—Jack Lemmon

It's been over a week since our heart-to-heart. It's crazy, but ever since Ford basically said he didn't want me anymore, I can't stop thinking about him.

I watch the ocean roar, curling in perfect corduroy lines toward the coast. Waves are hella good today. Perfect sets. And Ford is standing next to me as we watch the ocean crash toward us.

It's not a beginner day. The wind whips my hair around. Today, Turmo feels like a wild place, and I'm a wild thing coming home. Ford zips my wetsuit, which sends a million little tingles down my spine. I whirl around, forgetting everything but the way I feel right now. The way I've felt the past few days. Yeah, we talked and made our peace. We said all the right words, but all the right words in the world couldn't erase the unspoken tension we constantly juggle or ignore. It's like the only way to get past this wasteland of words-not-said is to pull him to me and kiss him. Just do it already and release the tension. I want to pull his face down to mine, and lean in until his lips are so close we're millimeters apart.

Something snaps and I realize what I'm doing. I step back and clear my throat and futilely try to throw some distance between us. I say, "Better get the boards waxed. Don't want to miss out on the surf."

Ford pulls at the collar of his wetsuit. "Um, yeah."

Confused, I bend down to work on my board. I say, "Are you ready for the Pumphouse?"

"I was planning on surfing the Point today."

I pop up to standing in a flash. "I'm not ready to surf the Point."

"Yeah, you are. C'mon, it's not the same when we surf different breaks."

I take a deep breath and look at fierce waves blasting the Point; the sets are never-ending. Thanks to some crazy weather, the waves are freakin' epic and everyone's out today. "I don't know."

Ford checks out the surf and grins. He reaches over and gives my shoulder a quick rub. That's it; all he has to do is touch me. That spot his hand touched feels hot, like every inch of my skin is dry tinder, ready to catch fire.

He says, "I do know, and you're ready. Don't you need

to practice the big waves for the comp? What is it, like four weeks away?"

I duck my head and wax my board. It's like his touch scrambled my brain, my heart, my existence.

"Look, Grace. It's not like you have to surf the Point. It's just I know you can totally kick butt out there."

"I wish I knew. I'm gonna sit on the shoreline and watch for a while. If I'm feeling brave, maybe I'll paddle out. I need a moment to psych myself up." I hug myself, unsure if I've got what it takes.

Ford's eyes linger on me for a moment before he attaches his leash.

"Remember it's a northwest swell today," I tell him. "Watch out for rip currents. It's high tide, so you've got a limited window before the rocks become a problem."

He nods and grabs his board, leaving me behind with a slight nod of the head. He marches out to the five-foot swells like they're nothing. I swallow and watch, wishing I had the guts to follow him. Sometimes I feel like I'm living life on the sidelines, and sometimes I get this totally ballsy mentality and go for it. I wish this was one of those times. What will happen if there are epic waves on comp day? I'll turn paddlepuss and back out?

It's times like this I'm not so sure I'm a winner. Not so sure I deserve anything. Lately, I'm feeling even more like I'm walking through a minefield—at home, everywhere—waiting for the eventual step when everything blows up in my face.

Ford's confidence makes me nervous, but I guess when you're surfing a more advanced spot, you have to own it.

When he hits the shoreline, he turns around and gives me a surfs-up hand gesture, his middle fingers curled in with his thumb and pinky pointing out. I sign it back with a half smile.

He paddles out on a current, duck dives some big curls, and joins the crowd. The wind blows my hair around. I take a rubber band off my wrist and capture wild strands flying about getting knotted, and turn it into a high ponytail. Then I rest my chin on my knees and watch everyone else. Normally being at the beach is what makes me feel like I'm floating untethered by anything. Right now, I feel weighted down like rocks are tied to my ankles, like I'm at home. I'd been psyched to surf the Pumphouse, but the Point? You mess up, you get messed up—most likely by Grimace rock.

Today is turning out to be an ugly reality check. I'm not so sure I'm ready for the competition. Not so sure I *will* be ready. How am I ever going to pull this off if I'm too chicken to surf the Point?

A huge wave swells and three guys are lined up to fight it out. I'm sure they all think it's their time, their turn. Things will get territorial fast. Some guys will duke it out. Most don't. But even pacifists are likely to call the bro who bunked their wave an assmunch, or give him a dirty look.

The three dudes paddle hard to catch the wave at the sweet spot. It's all about timing. One of them gets sucked up to the top, which means he's going to get dropped hard and caught inside the wash. The other two bros catch it. They could stay out of each other's way, but then they wouldn't be able to pull the moves they want. Their boards come dangerously near each other, and after a brief shove they carve in different directions. Of course, one of them has the better side and totally dominates before he cuts out. The second guy flips the bird as his ride fizzles.

Other surfers show up, drifting on the beach, wandering toward the water, looking like they're still recovering from Friday-night parties. A blond guy blows chunks about fifteen feet behind me, near a trash can. Nasty. The retching sound is followed by, "Dude, can a bro get some water?"

I turn around, watching in grotesque fascination. His friend keeps waxing the board. "Chuuuuf. Sorry, dude. You backwash."

Hangover Guy asks, "Got any gum?"

"What do I look like, a freakin' gas station?"

I chuckle silently to myself and dig into my bag to find some gum. I turn back around and lob a few pieces of Bubble Yum in their direction. "Hey, catch."

Hangover Guy misses by a few feet and trudges over to sweep the gum out of the sand. "Thanks."

I laugh. "Wouldn't want your breath to attract sharks."

Gas Station Guy cackles. "Dude, the femme totally saved your butt *and* ripped you a new one."

I grin. This kind of back-and-forth is part of what makes the surfer crowd fun. This is the world where I belong. Not with my mom and her stupid tailored shorts. Not with my dad and his need for a spotless house and total control. These people get me.

Hangover Guy pops the gum into his mouth. "Yeah,

but can the femme jazz the glass or does she only play in the foamies?"

Now he's ticking me off, pushing my buttons in a way only Ford can get away with. But I'm stuck like gum on the sidewalk. Because it's true. Today, I'm shunning beautiful glass swells to watch from the shoreline. And if I were planning on surfing any part of the Point, I'd probably surf the foamies. Leftovers on the edge of the break are a bit calmer.

His buddy tucks a small bit of wax into the calf of his wetsuit. "Dude. Femmes *always* surf foamies. Real bros surf the big dogs."

Then he heads out to the ocean without a backward glance, leaving me steaming on the beach.

Mr. Hangover cackles and says, "Ouch. Later, diva. Spanks for the gum."

I sit on the beach fuming. There are so many surfer girls that shred as hard or harder than most guys. Those chumps are 1950s in the worst way. Sexist. Some spark of anger inside me fans my competitive side. I'm going to show those tools what's up. They think I don't have what it takes? I can hang with them. I'll prove it.

I wax my board with a vengeance, focusing on building up a thick coat. Then I comb it, attach my leash, and march out to the ocean, my bare feet stomping across the hot sand. It feels like my heart is pumping blood ninety miles an hour. I zone in on the current I've seen everyone paddle out on. The lineup is full of surfers dotting the horizon. I guess I'll find Ford after I paddle out.

I take a deep breath and speed into the water, enjoying

the sound of the slap-down when my board hits a wave rolling under it.

Huge waves crash over me and I gasp for breath every chance I get. Maybe this is suicide. I paddle harder than I ever have to stay on the board and keep moving forward.

The next set gains momentum and I paddle as fast as I can until I reach calmer water. My arms may be noodled, but I'm stoked that I made it. I sit tall on my board and flash the Chumps a *what the heck do you know* look.

It's a sausage fest. A bunch of guys make catcalls and whistle. Ford swims over. The pride on his face melts me. It makes the accomplishment of getting out to the lineup that much sweeter.

"I knew you'd make it. You just needed a little time to get your edge on."

"Yeah, something like that." I bristle when I think of the idiots who implied girls pretty much suck. I'll show them girls can rip as hardcore as guys.

We straddle our boards and wait. After an eon of watching other surfers rip hard, it's our turn. My heart climbs into my throat. I hadn't really thought this far.

Ford yells, "Go for it! Paddle, paddle, paddle."

And I do. But not hard enough. Realizing I'm too late, I lean back, grab the board nose up, and cut out so the wave doesn't take me. I spin around to look at Ford. What am I doing out here? Besides royally screwing up?

Some guy with a buzz cut says, "Hey femme, no time for foreplay. Go to the back of the line."

If I get called femme one more time today…

Ford gives him the stink-eye. "Ignore the douche. You can have my go. See the second bump of the next set. Your name's written all over it."

That gets me—right in the gut. Ford's giving up his wave for me.

The chach behind Ford says, "Nice for you your boyfriend is giving you his spot. If you chuf this one, you won't be that lucky with me."

"Shove it, bro." Ford flips him the bird. Then he turns and looks me dead in the eye, full of intensity. "It's all you, Grace."

I nod and shake out my arms. I can do this. Once I catch the sweet spot, I'll be golden. My moment comes, Ford gives my board a push, and I go for it. Thanks to pure luck, I catch the wave and feel my board propel forward on a rush of water.

As the wave crests, the momentum freaks me out. I prepare to drop in, and pop up too soon. The powerful suction pulls my board down the face, straight to the bottom. I'm standing, but I gotta ease back fast. The nose of my board points downward. I drop low and grab the edge to force a maneuver hard left. I add weight to my back left foot, crouching low. The board nosedives forward and I fly off the side.

Falling. Quick breath. Water crashes on top of me with the force of a cabin cruiser. I plunge downward. *Shit, the rocks.* I tumble in so many directions, I have no clue which way is up. The snap of my surfboard being pulled in the opposite direction yanks my ankle, hard, searing into my skin. I try to grab my leg, but I can't get my hands down there. After a few more seconds of pain, the leash breaks free. My board. Shit. I'm screwed. Lights flash through my head. I need air. I fight my way, trying to find the top. Can't hold breath much longer. I burst through the waterline. Deep breath. Another wave crashes hard. Down, down I swirl. This time I'm pushed forward and down.

Bam. I slam into something hard—rocks. Sharp pain grates my skin. I cover my face and head with my arms. The current lets up; I kick hard to swim to the top.

If I don't make it to the surface, if someone isn't there... lungs burn. My body hurts, but a surge of adrenaline helps me swim to the top. I think it's the top. Can't tell anymore. As I break the surface, I hear people yelling. I'm exhausted and trying to figure out where to swim, but the saltwater burns my eyes. A surfboard makes a beeline toward me, but I can't focus so great and I'm doggie paddling just to keep my head above water.

A few more minutes, I tell myself. *I can make it*. Maybe. The board reaches me, and a pair of strong arms hoists me up, drags me onto something. A surfboard. Not mine. I don't think. I don't even know who the guy is, but I feel his weight on me as he paddles toward the shore. It's comforting.

He says, "It'll be okay. Hang in there a few more minutes."

I don't say anything. I lie there, eyes closed. Wanting sleep. I love the floating sensation of being on a board. I could drift here forever.

In a deep voice, he says, "We're almost there. I'm gonna walk you in." Then I feel a little shake and that soothing voice becomes abrupt. "Hey, are you okay? Stay with me. Open your eyes."

But I don't want to open my eyes. Drifting. Away from everything. Sounds so good.

I feel the weight of his arm across my waist. Then he lifts me off the board and I'm weightless as he cradles me in his arms. The *thunk thunk* of his walk jostles me. I wince. I was rescued by an ogre.

I whisper-croak, "Head hurts."

"I'm sure it does, girlie. Bitch as much as you want; don't go to sleep."

Thunk, thunk. Jostle, jostle. Torture.

He stops and lays me down on the sand. A sea of voices buzz like a swarm of angry bees. It hurts my head so much. Someone peels my eyes open and shines a bright light in. I try to pull back, but the sand has me hemmed in.

I attempt to sit up, but my shoulders are pressed back into the sand. Someone holds a towel to my forehead. Why is there a crowd of people around? It's not like I'm that important. Besides, if I can survive seventeen years in my house, what's it matter if I get sucked over the falls?

"Everybody back the hell off." The big blurry guy speaks sharply, motioning at my audience.

"The rest of you back way the hell off. I'm not going anywhere. She's my girl."

Ford. He's here. His girl? My brain feels scrambled, but I like the sound of that.

"Grace, baby, open your eyes. Help us out here."

His voice feels safe. It floods me with relief. I force my eyes open. He lifts a tangle of wet hair out of my face. I whisper, "Hey."

sixteen

remorse: *a gnawing distress arising from a sense of guilt for past wrongs* —www.merriam-webster.com

Grace yawns, sprawled out across my living-room couch. "I'm cashed out. I'm not dying. Quit with the twenty questions and quit being so anal about keeping me awake."

How can she be so irritating and lovable at the same time? "You could have fooled me. I was flipping out when Kahuna Pete paddled you in. You were *limp* when he carried you onto the beach. You barely responded at first. Gave me a freakin' aneurism. If I hadn't promised to take stellar care of you, they might have swung in the direction of the hospital instead of bringing you here. I swore I would keep a tight watch over you."

She shields her eyes from nearby lamplight. I rush to turn it off. She peeks out from under her hand sheepishly.

"Okay, okay. Sorry. It's just … my head hurts and I feel like I've been run over by an eighteen-wheeler."

I look at her, concerned. And part of me wonders if she was with it enough to hear me say she was my girl. Total slip. Just got caught up in the drama of the moment. We're not anything. Period. I pat her knee. Then I stand up, hands in my pockets. "Do you want *migas*? PB&J?"

"Do you have any rice, or cheese and crackers?" She closes her eyes for a second. She looks so helpless laid out on my couch. "And maybe some water?"

Guilt hits me like a Mack truck. I slap my forehead. "Of course, you want water. What was I thinking?"

I run through the kitchen like guys raiding it on Superbowl Sunday. In minutes I'm juggling a plate of cheese and crackers, PB&J on a separate plate, and a glass of water.

Grace winces out a smile. I feel like a jerk. Shouldn't have taken her to the Point. I pushed her too hard. Her dad is going to be *pissed*.

She says, "Wow. Now that's service. Maybe I should get shredded at the Point more often."

Ouch. To my core. "Not funny. I'm really sorry about that. I shouldn't have pushed you into it."

She sets down the cracker. "You didn't. I got annoyed by a couple of guys teasing me and wanted to prove them wrong. Instead, they probably think I'm a total kook."

I snort … of all things for her to be worried about right now. Typical Grace. "Who cares what they think? I'll tell you what I think. Surfing the Point was a bad idea. We'll stick with other breaks. Cool?"

She sips water and then frowns. "Not cool. I'm not giving up. I'm going to paddle back out there and catch a stupid wave. I can do it. I messed up on my timing. Come on. I'm serious about joining a surf team. You think the college coach is going to want someone who says, 'Excuse me, sir, I'm too wussy to surf this break. I'll work on blah blah blah a few jetties down.' Yeah, right. Paddlepusses don't make the big leagues."

I slide my hands down my face and stop at my cheeks. "*Ai, Mamacita*. What am I going to do with you?"

"Keep me. And let's start training again. Harder this time."

"Harder?" I only get to surf with her like three times a week. How is that going to happen?

"Yeah. Don't go easy on me."

"You're not gonna like it." I drop my hands to my side and stare at the floor, wondering if I'll even get to go surfing with her again. Mr. Parker was clear about his expectations for protecting Grace from other guys; I'm pretty sure protecting her from rocks at the Point would be implied in the general agreement. I'm in Shitville, pretty much. And genius that I am? I drove there myself.

Grace grabs my hand. It's like she's lightning and I'm thunder. One touch and I'm ready to roar. She rubs her little fingers across my thumb and says, "That's okay, 'cause I like you."

I burrow next to her on the couch, dying at the awkwardness of this situation. She's got to cool off—she's always so hot and cold. First we're a no-go for a lunch date, then cozy at Huntington, then off at the bonfire, then hot as all get-out this morning, and now she's about to make me come unglued.

"What can I say to that?" I ask.

"Yes."

"Fine. But we'll wait a week for you to recover. Deal?"

"Deal."

The front door clicks. Aw crap. Ma just got home from her morning girls' coffee. I wait quietly, hoping she won't go through the living room. Nope. No such luck. She takes one look at Grace on the couch, drops her purse, and speeds over.

She clucks over Grace. "*Mija.*" Then she turns accusing to me. "Good God, Ford, what did you let happen to this poor girl?"

I hang my head, annoyed and guilty. I don't want to look her in the eyes. She's right. I don't need her looks or scolding to know that I screwed up.

"Mrs. Watson, it wasn't his fault."

Out of the corner of my eyes, I can see Ma's hands fly up in the air. "It doesn't matter. You are my princess and he should guard you like royalty."

Join the club. Like I don't *know* that. I mutter, "I know, *Mammi.*"

Ma says, "Do your parents know about this yet?"

I look over at Grace. She starts to shake her head no, but ends up clenching her eyes shut.

I sit up and stare Ma in the eyes. "You're stressing her out."

Ma grabs a blanket and puts it on Grace. Another thing I didn't do. She says, "Let me know if you need anything, *mija*." Then she shoots me a dirty look. I'll be getting an earful later.

seventeen

Champions keep playing
until they get it right.
—Billie Jean King

Ford and I decide that the best approach with my parents is to tell them as little as possible about today's events. So after dinner, Ford drives me home, unloads my surfboard, and drops me off at the front door. I'm wearing one of his too-big-for-me surfer jackets to cover my arms; it's my face that we can't cover up.

Right as I'm about to head in to face the firing squad, Ford makes a sign of the cross and runs around to the driver's seat. We'd agreed that if he came in it would seem like a bigger deal—he never comes inside my house after surf sessions.

He jumps into Esmerelda and bolts.

Jeeze, it's not like he'll go to prison or something. It

was my screw-up. I clap my flip-flops together to shake the sand off and leave them on the front porch.

I unlock the door to find my parents hanging out in the living room looking cozy. They're going through a good phase right now, which will hopefully work in my favor. Then I try to not hobble too noticeably as I cross the room.

Right as I'm about to round the corner, Mom says, "My God, what happened to your face?"

I stop. "Nothing really. I fell off my board and got a few minor scrapes. The lifeguard checked it out. Everything's okay."

"The lifeguard? Minor scrapes? You fell?" Mom is no longer relaxed or leaning against Dad; she's sitting up straight. "Your face has more Band-Aids covering it than skin showing, and you say everything's okay?" The loud, shrill tone in her voice makes my headache worse.

I clench my hands into fists at my side to keep from holding on to my head.

Mom rushes over to give me a hug, and when she pulls back, she examines the scratches on my face.

I pull back, annoyed. "It's nothing. I took a tumble…got sucked into the falls."

Mom rejoins Dad on the couch and grips his arm, a stressed look on her face. Dad eyes me with a semi-exasperated look of concern. "You're going to have to spill more than that to diffuse your mom's red alert signal. What the hell happened? Those Band-Aids are going to hurt like hell when you rip them all off."

I grin somewhat sheepishly. We'd swapped out a large

bandage covering several scrapes on my cheeks for lots of small, flesh-colored Band-Aids in hopes of attracting less attention. Now I know why Mama Watson clucked, shook her head, and wished me luck.

"Ford and I surfed the Point at Turmo and I caught this epic wave, but my nose pushed downward and I flew off the board and got rolled into the wave. It was big waves today, so I hit bottom for a little bit before I came back up. Someone was there to help me out. The lifeguard checked me. I'm fine." I stop to catch my breath after rolling all that out without stopping.

Dad says, "The Point? You know better than to surf that. It's not a beginner break."

I huff. "And I'm not a beginner. Besides, how can I get better if I don't surf harder waves?"

Mom scoots to the edge of the couch. "You won't get better because you won't be surfing any more waves. I've never liked you surfing. And what about your future? College? What if you'd really gotten hurt?" She turns to my father. "And you—you helped get her into this mess."

Dad scoots back. He does a double take between Mom and me.

"Are you kidding me?" I say. "I'm almost eighteen. You can't ban surfing." My head is pounding and my face hurts from talking so much. "I'm ahead on all my studies. I'm number one in the class. What more do you want? My college apps in blood? This is crazy."

"Whoa," Dad says. "Everybody slow down here. Elaine, don't you think you're overreacting?"

"Overreacting? Our daughter comes home with her beautiful face all scraped up and I'm out of line? I don't think so." She turns on me, her face a bright pink, and points her finger at me. "What if you got knocked out or brain-damaged? There goes the Ivy League. There goes your future. Don't expect me to take care of you when you're a quadriplegic in diapers. Ask your dear old dad or one of your surfing buddies. Do you think Ford's going to stand by and feed you carrots through a straw the rest of his life? Because I don't."

"Grace is plenty ladylike, and she needs some sort of physical activity besides school," Dad says. "She needs an outlet. And for God's sake, she's not going to end up a quadriplegic. Let's chill out on the melodramatics." He turns his body toward Mom and scoots over until their legs touch. "Can't we find a middle ground? She knows her limits now. Right, Grace?"

I bite my lip and nod. Ouch—I forgot my lip is cut.

Mom tears up. "How? I don't want someone knocking on our door saying my baby drowned."

Dad puts his arm around her and she collapses into him, sniffling. I understand her being worried, but I wish she got the irony of her concern for my physical welfare. She worries about the beach, but what about Dad's tirades?

Dad points to a nearby chair for me to sit in. I sit and wait, my heart in my throat and my lifeline in his hands.

He says, "How about if Grace doesn't surf the Point again—"

"But—" I start.

"Don't interrupt when I'm helping you," he growls.

I shrink, nodding silently.

"How about she not surf the Point anymore? And she takes a break from surfing this next week? That gives her time to heal and you time to relax." He looks back and forth between us. "Deal?"

I say, "Deal." Then I keep my mouth shut. Besides, I have to sit this week out anyway.

Mom shrugs and says, "I wash my hands of this. Don't come to me for sympathy if you get hurt again."

Dad shoos me out of the room. Before he turns his attention back to Mom, he gives me a wink.

I slink down the hall, grateful and determined not to screw up the next time I surf the Point.

eighteen

chilaquiles: *fried tortilla chips*
with eggs, salsa, and cheese

Ai. Mr. Parker's going to let me have it. I'm screwed. For
once I comb my hair. Like that's going to save me. I dropped
Grace off on her porch Saturday night with a face that looked
like it had road rash. And it was my fault. Well, maybe not
totally. But I took her there. I didn't paddle out with her. I
wasn't nearby when she got thrashed. A clear-cut case of neg-
ligence. Case closed. My ass is grass. Good-bye future internship hookups.

I run my hand across my jaw. Then I trudge to the
kitchen as if one of Ma's cast-iron skillets is hanging around
my neck. The smell of *chilaquiles* perks me up. One of my
favorites.

"Coffee's in the French press." Ma waves a hand toward

my mug. Then she goes back to stirring fried tortilla strips, onion, and eggs. "Hand me the hot sauce, *mijo*."

I grab the jar of salsa she made yesterday. My mouth is watering. "So what's the occasion? "

"Your impending head on a platter." She dumps half the sauce into the pan, where it will simmer until it's thick. Man, I love that smell.

"Gee thanks, Ma." I pick at the cheese waiting to melt over it all. "You gonna show at my funeral?"

She swats my hand away. "Pour yourself some coffee. And *mijo*? Refill mine, *por favor*."

"Yes ma'am." I sit at the bar.

She turns toward me, waving a wooden spoon. "You need *chilaquiles* this morning."

I sip black coffee. "Yeah. I do."

"So how are you planning on handling this?"

I shrug. "Don't know."

She sprinkles cheese over the skillet in a circular pattern. Always making things look good. "*Mijo*. You find Mr. Parker. Tell him you are sorry. And then stand there and take what you have coming." She raises an eyebrow. "Within reason." She takes the skillet off the stove and sets it on a hot pad near me.

I reach out and pick off a gooey tortilla strip. "*Ai, caliente*." I blow on it fast a few times before popping it in my mouth. Then I tuck it to the side so my tongue doesn't get too burnt to enjoy breakfast.

Ma whacks me on the head. I pull back grinning. She says, "Use a plate."

I slide her coffee cup to her. "It was only a little piece."

She hones in on me. "A plate, *mijo*."

That *mijo* wasn't the term of endearment. It was the warning one. The *I'm your mama and I can take you out* kind. I make a big show of walking over to the cabinets and pulling out two plates. I hand Ma one.

"Madam. May I serve you *chilaquiles*? I heard the cook is exceptional."

She chuckles. "You're too much, *mijo*."

"Ah. Now that *mijo* is music to my ears." I scoop a small portion onto her plate, teasing her.

She makes a big show with her hands and winks. "That's the perfect amount. For a single-celled amoeba! Give me a real portion."

I shovel a large serving on her plate. After plopping two giant scoops on my plate, I say, "Thanks, Ma."

She nods and pats my arm. "You're a good boy, Ford. It'll work out."

———————

I walk into the office ten minutes early.

Teresa looks down her glasses at me. "Mr. Parker wants to see you."

I stop short, hovering my soon-to-be nonexistent butt over the chair. "Might as well get it over with, right?"

She frowns at me, concerned. "*Que paso?*"

"I screwed up. Took his daughter surfing at a place she wasn't ready for … apparently. Her face looks like it got in a fight with a meat grinder."

Teresa gasps.

"Well, I might be exaggerating a little bit."

She whispers, "It was nice working with you, Ford."

My head drops. I haven't even thought about getting fired. I've been more focused on the getting-reamed-out part. My folks don't yell, but since I'm dealing with a lawyer, I expected a verbal assault of sorts. Not getting canned. I whisper, "My rec letter."

"Let me know if you need anything," Teresa says. "Recommendations. Anything."

"Thanks." Man, this is too heavy. I straighten up and comb at my bangs. Teresa gives me a strange look. Then I grin. "Might as well look good when my head's on the chopping block. I mean, I am a pretty boy."

She smiles back. "I don't know what to do with you. *Buena suerte*, Ferdinand."

"*Gracias*." I walk tall down the hallway. I'm a Caudillo. Well, a Caudillo-Watson. We don't tuck tail and run.

I knock on Mr. Parker's office door.

"Come in."

I walk right in. "Excuse me, sir? Could we talk about this weekend?"

He gives me a disgruntled look. He's puffed up like a rooster at a cockfight. Looks like the man version of Grace when she gets ready for a fight. It's kind of funny.

He says, "Well, I sure as hell didn't invite you in here to shoot the breeze."

Whoa. Starting off easy. "I'm sorry about Grace's accident," I say. "Sorry about not walking her inside—she thought it would make things worse. But I shouldn't have dropped her off on the front porch without taking the heat with her. That's been bothering me."

A little air goes out of him. "Well, I'm glad you can own up. Grace—she's my little girl. If I let someone take her out surfing, I expect that person to take care of her. We made a deal. Perhaps I didn't make myself clear, but part of watching out for her includes not taking her to the Point and then letting her fend for herself. She could have been … Well, you and I both know she's damn lucky."

I force myself to look him in the eye. "Yes sir."

"You ever play poker, Ford?"

I resist the urge to loosen my collar. "Yes sir."

"You know what happens to people who welch on their bets?"

I clear my throat. "No sir."

He leans forward. "They get kicked out of the game. How do you feel about that?"

"Not too hot, sir."

"Her mother doesn't want her to surf again. Ever." He sits behind his desk, comfortable. Holding all the cards.

That's bogus. No way would Grace quit surfing. "How do you feel about that, sir, being a former surfer yourself?" I ask.

"That's a good question, Counsel. I'm not in favor of that."

This is a game to him. Reaming me out. Making me sweat. It's bullshit. I pull my shoulders back. "And what would you be in favor of?"

"Grace needs to take a week off. She needs to focus on college applications. She needs some time away from the waves. I don't want her getting right back out there. She could use a little time to develop some healthy fear. The ocean's big stuff, son. It demands respect. Something you both seem to be short on."

I grit my teeth before asking, "Where do we go from here?"

He gets a hard look on his face. "Grace doesn't surf the Point. And you keep a better watch on her if you want to continue to be surfing buddies. Now, there's just one other thing I need to talk to you about." He pauses, staring at me with narrowed eyes. "I may work long hours, but I know there's somebody taking her out on the days you're in my office. Who is it?" He leans in, his face worried. "There's nothing going on there, right?"

I shove my hands in my pockets and ball them into fists. I remind myself he's helped a lot of people—my people. Then I smile like everything's golden. He's not firing me; he's playing cat and mouse. And yeah, I might deserve to sweat a little. I dropped Grace off injured without even walking her in. That was pretty much asking for it.

"Damien?" I answer. "Not a chance anything's going on there, not if I have anything to do with it. Is that all, sir?"

He leans back into his chair. "For now." Then he does that whole two fingers from his eyes to me, the *I'm watching you* sign, which would be funny if it were a joke.

nineteen

It's all about where your mind's at.
—Kelly Slater

"C'mon. Ten more."

"Are you nuts?" I fall flat on a beach towel, my face to the side. "I've already done fifty. I hate push-ups."

"Your point?"

"They suck. Yours?"

Ford cops a squat closer to me, shuffling sand onto my towel. He leans over my face, which is still scabbed up. "The perfect wave, on a kickass day at the Point. You kicking butt and taking names at the Crazy John's Surf Comp. You having the stamina and strength to know you can stick it."

This week, I've been relegated to watching from the shore—part of the crummy taking-a-break-from-surfing deal. It's only been a few days, but I'm fine now. A little sore. Like there's any point to this time off besides the fact that it's torture to watch from the sidelines. I groan and grunt through ten more push-ups.

When I flop back down, I just lie there facing the water lapping the shore. I space out and dream about catching a wave at the Point and not getting raked over Grimace rock. I know I got really lucky. There's no room for luck, though. It's all about skill and commitment. The day I got caught under, I didn't fully commit, and that was a painful mistake. But how does a person figure out when to listen to their gut, when fear is in the way, and when they should go for it?

"Grace."

I roll onto my back and squint up at Ford. "Yeah?"

"Are you ready to run?" He dangles worn blue running shoes over my stomach before dropping them at my side. "For the record, you've got game. I'm just helping you figure it out."

Instead of saying anything, I toss the shoes to the side. I readjust my ponytail and hop up before Ford can get his shoes on. I start off with a full-out sprint and eventually slow down to a steady jog. The *thunk thunk* rhythm relaxes me. The burn in my calves feels good. For whatever reason, there's something comforting about the ache that comes with pushing my limits. Maybe because it dulls the pain I can't fix. Kind of like stomping on someone's foot to help a headache. The headache doesn't go away, but they darn sure become more concerned with their toes.

Ford lopes along behind me, keeping his distance, understanding my need for space. He's my personal godsend. I focus on the feel of the sand giving way beneath my feet. Seagulls scatter in front of me as I cut through them. They dot the air with color and sound before fluttering back to the ground in search of some kid's crumbs left behind. A light offshore wind carries the smells of salt and sea creatures. Everything about the beach is predictable, and not. It's a thousand variations of an ocean concerto. It's music that can't be captured by notes on stanzas. It's perfect.

At the end of our run, I fall back on the sand. Out of breath. Blood whooshing through my ears. That's my kind of run. Stop when you drop.

Ford plops down beside me. He's sitting up. I shade my eyes with my hand and squint up at him. My breathing is calming down but my pulse isn't. Ever since I heard him say *she's my girl* at the Point, my insides go into overdrive when we're near each other.

———

Every month our church pulls together for a community service day. Instead of going to church, people sign up for a volunteer activity. This go-round, Mom signed our family up to serve food at a homeless shelter. So I show up at breakfast in a long-sleeved T-shirt and my favorite pair of worn Roxy jeans. They're so comfy, and I like the way they fray at the ends.

Mom's right eyebrow rises. "Tell me you're changing before church?"

Dad glances up from his bowl of oatmeal and looks me over. I take a deep breath and focus on keeping my mouth closed.

"Grace?"

Ack. She wants an answer.

"Well, I was planning on wearing this to the Give Fest today."

She taps manicured nails on the table. "What does that say about you?"

Tap, tap, tap. Dad looks back and forth between us.

"Um, it says I like comfortable clothes. And besides, if I were to get all dressed up, it might make the folks we're serving feel uncomfortable." My T-shirt is a classic plain shirt and besides, it's even got a boat-neck cut—which is sort of dressy.

Tap, tap, tap. Huff.

I'm silent during our little fashion standoff.

Dad looks at both of us again. "Oh come on, Elaine. She's got a point about not overdressing. Besides, she's a teenager—aren't they supposed to wear worn jeans? If she shows up in a dress or pantsuit, she'd be ostracized. And she'll be serving food, anyway—wearing an apron. People won't notice anything but her smile and whether or not she gives 'em a good serving of mashed potatoes." He grins. "So represent the Parker family well. No skimping on the taters."

Tap, tap, tap. Mom throws her hands up in the air. "Fine. I give up. You win." She makes her exit from the kitchen muttering, "Worn jeans to church."

I shift back and forth.

Dad grins at me and whispers, "She'll get over it."

I grin back and mouth, "Thanks."

At the shelter, everyone bustles about adding last-minute decorations, repositioning welcome banners, and gabbing. My mom laughs while balancing on a chair and hanging corny summer decorations. Dad's chatting it up with other men while they finish lining up chairs around the tables. I enjoy the warmth of the kitchen as I help organize the serving dishes and plastic silverware. We look like the perfect family.

Mrs. Franks, a sweet old lady in her eighties, is in charge of the food. Or at least she's one of the helpers. She's a doll and naturally takes over. I guess after eighty years of living and raising her own family, she knows how to get food on a table.

"Grace, could you help me out with the drink table?" Mrs. Frank's voice warbles toward me.

"Sure thing, Mrs. Franks." I speed over to help the doddering woman before she disappears behind the five-gallon tea dispenser. I think she'll tip over sideways.

After securing the tea dispenser, I ask, "Where would you like it?"

She points her faded papery hand to the far right end of the table.

I set it down. "Does that look okay to you?"

"A little bit closer to the center, dear. We don't want it falling off the edge, and you can call me Sister Franks like everyone else." She pats my back after I've adjusted the beast.

"Okay, Sister Franks." I force the words from my mouth.

It feels a bit odd, but she's from a different time period so I roll with it.

Under her supervision, I set up the drink table to perfection, placing the last cup on the plastic red-checked tablecloth. Some kid runs through the room announcing our guests' arrival.

Somehow Sister Franks and I have decided to be buddies for the day. So we stand next to each other serving mashed potatoes and green bean casserole. It's fun scooping the mashed potatoes on plates for the sea of faces passing by me. And Sister Franks is off the charts. She has something to say to everyone.

"My, my, young man. I think a growing boy like you might need an extra scoop." She winks at him.

"Oh, what a pretty dress you're wearing." The little girl's face lights up and the tired mom smiles for a brief second.

Watching Sister Franks love on folks renews my faith in people. After an hour of this, I realize she means every word she's saying. What a sweet old lady.

Every now and then I search the crowded room for Mom and Dad. Every time I spot them, they're helping someone, cleaning up, or listening to one of our guests. Every time I inspect their faces, they look happy. My parents get so excited about helping people; I know this is one of the reasons they decided to attend this church.

A guy from the youth group stops by to say, "Jeesh, Grace. Your dad is hilarious. You're so lucky."

I nod and give a tight smile. "Yep, that's me. Lucky Grace."

A lump builds in my throat. I wish this feeling could

extend to our family year-round. This happiness. This love. It's confusing, mixed up, and it hurts.

"Grace. This good-looking young man needs a big scoop of mashed potatoes." Sister Franks' voice pulls me out of lala land.

I grin at a scruffy guy in his twenties. "Sorry about that."

He smiles. "No problem. I know that look. Cheer up. Things can't be that bad." He moves on with his tray.

I look after him, startled. Am I that transparent? Surely not. If I was, people would have figured out my charade by now. No, this guy knows what it means to want something you can't have. And here he is, encouraging me. I feel like the crumb that I am. So I paint a smile on my face, determined to love on folks like Sister Franks does.

twenty

Daaaamn: *like a really emphasized wow;*
can be use to express almost any
emotion including admiration

Transcribing affidavits is like working on those little puzzles in the kids magazines I got growing up. There were all these little blanks with symbols underneath, and you'd look up the symbol to figure out which letter went in the blank. Only affidavits are way crazy, and there aren't any blanks. It's frying my brain. All of these have to be translated from shorthand into English. Whoever created shorthand was nuts. I think it'd be way easier to just write things out.

I take a break to wipe my hands across my face and blink my eyes a few times. I run my hands through my hair and stare off at the ceiling.

"That bad, huh?" Brianna's soft voice pulls me back to reality.

I grin, sheepishly. "On a scale of one to ten with ten being equal to being scraped over Grimace Rock? I'd give it a nine." Then I bat my eyelashes at her. "I need a few minutes to space out. Don't turn me in. Pretty pleeeeease?"

She throws her head back and laughs. Full-on belly laugh. Then she pushes at my shoulder. "That's what works for little girls."

"Sexist."

"Never. In fact, would you like to go on a date tonight?" Brianna's face remains calm, as if girls ask guys out all the time.

Daaaamn. That's hot. I'm in. "Why yes I would, fair queen. Where?"

She pouts her lips. "A queen should not do all the work."

I smile and bow.

———————

As Brianna and I walk underneath the neon-lit awning and open the doors, a blast of stale popcorn and pizza hits us. The sounds of bowling balls thudding against wood lanes ricochet off the concrete walls.

I head straight to the counter where a Blue Hair waits to ring us up. She's gotta be in her seventies. According to her nametag, she's Gladys.

I say, "Hi ma'am. We'd like to rent a lane for the next couple of hours. We'll need the works—shoes, balls, gutter blockers." I shift my eyes back and forth before giving a loud stage-whisper. "She's a total newb."

"Well, I'll be darned." She winks at Brianna and doesn't even acknowledge me. "You let old Gladys fix you up. The first experience is always important."

Brianna laughs and thumps my elbow. "We don't need gutter blockers."

I give her a wide-eyed innocent look. "Are you sure?"

She puts her hands on those killer hips.

"She doesn't need the blockers," I say. "I guess we'll only need the shoes and balls."

Gladys laughs a raspy smoker's laugh and rings me up. "Okay, sugar. You're lane thirty. You let old Gladys know if you need anything else. You can pick out your shoes over there, and the balls are across from the lanes."

We grab retro shoes that reek of disinfectant. Then we head to our lane. We've got the last one, by the wall. It's been painted graffiti style with a mural of old famous people like Marilyn Monroe, Elvis, and Buddy Holly.

I turn around and fling my arm toward a rack of balls a few feet away. "Why don't you step into my office?"

"I'd love to," Brianna says.

Feeling like a king, I walk over and check out the goods. I grab a lime-green fifteen-pounder. Brianna hovers over a couple of balls before choosing an orange eight-pounder. I wiggle my eyebrows up and down. "You ready to get schooled?"

She swishes her hips as we walk back to our lane. "Don't get too cocky, Mr. Watson. I might surprise you."

"Let me have it. No holding back."

She laughs. "Oh, don't you worry about that."

I set up the computer system, keying in the monikers *Linda* and *El Toro*, which mean "pretty" and "the bull."

Brianna says, "What's that?"

I grin, forgetting she's doesn't speak Spanish. "What? I'm half Mexican. This is my cultural twist on Beauty and the Beast. *Linda* means pretty."

She smiles. "All right, *Toro*. Show me what you got."

I say, "Who says I'm *Toro*? Kidding."

I snag my ball and swagger toward the lane. *Thunk*. It hits the wood with a loud thud and rolls straight down the middle. Two thirds of the way down, it starts curving toward the gutter.

"It's all part of the plan," I say. "Watch and learn."

Then the ball curves back at the last second and knocks two pins down.

"All part of the plan, eh?" Brianna bumps me with her hips.

I'm having trouble focusing.

I wait at the ball return, finally able to come up with something witty. "Humble beginnings make victory taste that much sweeter." I grab the ball as it pops out of the chute and approach the lane holding the ball in both hands. I stand at the edge, widen my stance, and bend down, swinging the ball back between my legs and tossing it gently down the center. It wobbles down the middle and ends up knocking down all but one remaining pin. I turn to Brianna, waiting for a response. She winks and gives a small nod of appreciation. I pull my arms back, fist tightened, in a *yeah baby* motion and take a seat. "You're up, Buttercup."

Brianna grabs her ball like she knows exactly what she's doing. She walks like a queen toward the lane, stops at the edge, flings her arm back and releases the ball too early. It makes a loud thud and rolls toward me. I stop it with my feet. Then I howl with laughter.

Brianna shrugs her shoulders. "Humble beginnings, right?"

"I'm thinking that's along the lines of inglorious or mea-ger or infamous."

"Thanks."

"Anytime."

She gets the ball and heads back toward the lane. I walk up beside her and say, "Okay, it's time for a mini-lesson."

She puts a hand on her hip and waits.

I say, "Watch me act it out in slow motion." She watches my exaggerated walk and fake release, looking antsy to do it herself. "Notice, I didn't stop and then toss. It's all one fluid movement. You want to keep your thumb pointing straight. If your thumb points to the right, then the ball is likely to roll in that direction. Keep your elbow straight and slightly bend your left knee, which should be in front by the time you glide to the edge."

"Got it."

I say, "Let me walk you through it."

Then I stand so close I can smell her perfume. I reach for her right arm and guide her through the motion, my hand on the back of hers. As I swing her arm to the edge, I say, "Release now." Then I let go of her hand and step away fast, blood whooshing through my body. "You'll get it this time."

She says quietly, "Yep. Definitely. Thanks for the tip."

Then she knocks down eight pins. We high-five. "You rock!" I say.

By the final round, she's kicking my butt and loving every minute of it. We return our funky shoes to Gladys. She hands me a *buy one hour, get the second hour free* card. "Come again, honey. And bring your girlfriend."

And even though I'm not sure about the label, neither one of us corrects her.

twenty-one

Everything has to be rethought.
—Elias Canetti

The last prewashed dish clinks as Mom arranges it in the dish-washer. I grin, thinking about Mom's need to clean dishes by hand first.

> *The dishwasher isn't for scrubbing the dishes; it acts as a sterilizing agent.* —Mom

The dryer buzzes. "Grace, let's fold clothes and catch up on how things are going," she says.

The words by themselves sound inviting, but her tone is all business. Ugh. I head for the laundry room and transfer warm, lavender-scented laundry into a basket. I toss nearby hangers on top and trudge to the living room couch, which is our home base for folding and hanging clothes.

I grab a shirt and begin to fold it as meticulously as the clerks at Saks do.

Mom grabs a hanger and slips it underneath a shirt, from the bottom so as not to stretch the neck. "It seems like you've found a new surf partner for the days when Ford can't take you, but you and Ford have still been surfing together quite a bit."

I smooth out a wrinkle, ignoring the fact that she's fishing for information. "Yes ma'am."

She crinkles her forehead for a microsecond before smoothing it out with her fingers. "What about your college applications? Those essays won't write themselves."

I reach for a pair of panties and begin tri-folding them. "Umm. I figured I'd wait until school starts to do the final drafts, you know, run them past my English teacher? I've been focusing on filling out the basics on several."

"So you haven't finished any essays."

I open my mouth and hesitate. The answer: a flat-out lie. "Not final drafts, anyway. I've been playing around with the rough drafts and outlines."

She nods her approval.

I grab a shirt and focus on perfect creases. There isn't a right answer to the inquisition and, at this point, I can only make it worse.

"Grace?"

I look up at my mom, mid-crease.

She raises her eyebrows. "I'm counting on the fact you have enough sense not to get involved with Ford. He seems like a really nice guy, but with these surfer types—you really

171

need to watch it. They tend to be low on ambition. Wait for the Ivy League guys—you know they're good enough."

Wow. And um, hello? Surfers aren't all low on ambition, especially Ford. They just have *different* goals. Surf Pipeline. Travel the world. Go pro. Surf for life. Besides, we're in high school, give it up. Hardly anybody knows for reals what they want to do for the rest of their life.

"No problem," I tell her. "We're just friends. We're not dating. In fact, he takes other girls surfing."

Nothing about those statements feels right to me. I've been trying to ignore the incident with that Brittany girl, or whatever he name was, but I can't. My temples throb whenever I think about the possibility of another girl in Ford's life.

"That makes things easier." Mom pats my arm and gives it a small squeeze. "I hope you realize how much I love you. Don't lose sight of your priorities, everything you've worked for…you don't want to throw away the past three years of hard work to fail now. And the point of all your hard work is to get into the best college."

The best college? For who? Keeping sight of her priorities means losing sight of mine. Dreams keep slipping through my fingers like sand.

"Can you help me with the furniture?"

"Ah, man. Are you on a feng shui kick again?"

Mom power-walks to the other side of the couch, a woman on a mission. Her butt sticks out as she shoves the couch in a new direction, except the couch doesn't budge. She looks pretty funny; I can't help but laugh before lining up next

172

to her and giving a strong push. The behemoth inches forward.

"Thanks, honey." Mom turns and gives me a quick smile.

"No prob." I tuck a strand of hair behind my ear and push again. "What's with rearranging the furniture?"

"Nothing much. Your dad felt things were a bit staid, so I'm trying to up the energy in here." We have a good rhythm going on the couch and we're making progress.

"Are you serious?" I stop and twist around, popping my back.

Mom cringes at the snapping and crackling. "Grace, that gives me the heebie-jeebies."

I laugh. "Why don't you get Dad to move all this crap?"

"Right now isn't good timing. He's stuck on a pretty big case." She sighs. "It looks like this will be a tough win."

Translation: Stay out of his way.

I roll my eyes. Like that's anything new. Whatev. "Let's give this a final go."

Mom counts: "One, two, three, *push*."

The couch jolts forward and so do we. Mom ends up splayed across the end of it, rear end sticking up. All I hear is muffled laughter, since her face is buried in accent pillows. This is the mom I grew up with, the one who used to laugh more often. It seems like she laughs less every year. I miss that. I miss her. I miss the relationship we used to have— when I looked up to her as my hero. It seems like the older I get, the more my parents argue, and the more they argue, the harder she works and the less she smiles.

She comes up for air. "That should do it for now. We can move the recliner later. Think he'll like it?"

"What's with you and trying to make everything so *nice* for him? He treats us like crap one minute and queens the next." I'm sick of pretending. What's up with that?

Her happy face leaves the building. "Well, Grace," she snaps, "what do you want me to do? Huh? Leave him?"

"I don't know. Why not? You don't seem happy." I know I'm not.

"Then what? Marry someone else who treats me like crap? Learn how to put up with their crap? I think not."

Adrenaline pumps through me. The gloves are off. "How about marry someone who *doesn't* treat you like crap? Good guys do exist." I falter on the last line, wondering how many Fords are out there.

Mom's lips curl into a scowl. "Yeah, right. What do you know about life? Nothing."

"I know it *sucks* to be treated like I'm nothing." I want to explode, but my words come out in a carefully controlled tone. The edginess lies below the surface.

"Well, if I leave your father … what then? And what are you going to do? Be there for me? Oh wait, you're going off to college next year. I'll be all alone."

I don't know what to say to that. The shit of it is—she's right.

———

Not long after my argument with Mom, my cell rings. It's Damien.

He says, "Hey, baby. Wanna ride?"

I laugh. "Really? Is that the best you can do?"

"Made you laugh. Wanna catch a late-afternoon surf session? Turmo?"

I glance at the clock. "You know it."

"I'll swing by to pick you up in fifteen."

I start running around the room, yanking my shorts off while looking for my swimsuit. "I'll be ready in ten."

I barely make it to my front porch before Damien rolls up in my driveway, music blasting from his Jeep. I carry my Roxy duffel and board over to his vehicle. He slides my board on top of his and adjusts the strap so they don't rub against each other. I sit on the passenger side, enjoying how different his Jeep is from Esmerelda. It's immaculate. No stray pieces of trash in the floorboard. No marks on the dashboard. No rust on the paint job. It even has the new-car smell. I don't understand why Ford has such a problem with Damien. He has him all wrong.

Damien gets in and starts the car. No funny noises.

I say, "Once upon a time, I wouldn't have pictured you to be so orderly."

He turns down the radio. "That's when you didn't know me. I'm a man of surprise and mystery."

I lay on a sultry voice. "Ooh. Sexy."

He laughs. "You're a trip. Want to go out sometime?"

Whoa. He's straight to the point. "Um, you know I'm training for the comp. Trying to stay focused right now."

He says, "Oh, cool. I didn't realize you were so serious about this stuff. You need any help?"

"Yeah, totally. You've already been great helping me with my airs." But I feel guilty not mentioning Ford. So I add, "Ford's been helping me out too. Kind of my coach. But he's at his internship more often than not." Frustrated, I lean against the seat, feeling like more of an afterthought than a focus.

Damien says, "Dang. Ford gets around. He must be starting a surf school."

I stare out the window. What the heck *was* Ford doing with that... Brittany? My heart beats erratically and I feel sick. And there's nothing I can do to stop it.

Damien says, "You're quiet all of a sudden. What's up?"

"Nothing. I'm tired."

We get on the interstate. Damien turns the music louder. The windows are rolled down and between the wind and the music, there's no room for conversation. We're quiet the rest of the way to Turmo.

twenty-two

fold: *to stop playing
your hand, give up*

Warren Hollingsworth III matches his name in every way. He looks like he belongs on Cape Cod rather than sitting across from me and Hop at Lola's Coffee Shop. I wonder what dirt Jada has on him to get him to meet up with me.

He takes a sip of his green smoothie. "So, you and Jada must be pretty tight."

I shrug. Hop begins folding his napkin into a million little creases.

Hollingsworth leans forward. "She called in a favor. She doesn't do that."

I make a mental note to bust my ass extra for her the rest of the summer. I say, "Jada's a cool gal."

"Let's get to it." He leans in, resting his arms on his legs. "What's the situation with your friend?"

I say, "Hien came over from Vietnam when he was ten, and he's been living in San Diego ever since."

Warren says, "Why did his parents come here illegally? Why didn't they go through the proper channels?" He looks at Hop for an answer. So do I ... that hasn't been a burning question for me.

Hop stares at his sliver of napkin. "Religious persecution."

I blink, unsure of how to process that information. "What?"

Warren and I sit there waiting. Hop unfolds and refolds the napkin until he finally wads it into a ball and throws it on the table. He looks back and forth between me and Warren, a hard glint in his eyes. "They beat Hien and his parents. They said they had to renounce all religious activities, and they were not allowed to attend any sort of religious gathering."

My stomach twists into a sickened knot.

Warren drums his finger on the table. "We can work with that. People who come over illegally *without* persecution from their government are usually up a creek without a paddle in regards to obtaining legal status. They have to move back to wherever they came from and live there for who knows how long until they get approval, if they get approval. But most people don't leave their country on a whim. They usually are trying to find somewhere safer for their family or an economy that will provide them with better economic or educational opportunities. That's why some people just stay in the country illegally—it's in what they consider to be their best interests."

I'm sitting in my seat, frozen. Jorge didn't have a chance.

Warren asks Hop, "Do they have proof?"

Hop shrugs. "Other than a wicked scar by Hien's eye? I don't know."

Is that why Hien wears sunglasses all the time or why he dresses the way he does? Survival mode...

Warren says, "Well, that's the next step. Ask Hien if his parents have any hard proof. What is he—Unified Buddhist?"

"Yes," Hop says.

Feeling like an idiot, I ask, "How did you know that?"

"That's one of the main religions persecuted in Vietnam," Warren explains. "Check out the HRW report for 2005, which I'm guessing is the year Hien and his family arrived in San Diego."

"HRW?"

Hop fills in the blank. "Human Rights Watch."

I sink back in my chair, thinking I have way more to learn about immigration issues and laws than I could ever have imagined.

————

Hien's situation freaks me out. I don't know what to do, and I'm really glad Warren knows what's up. I exit the highway and take the familiar turns that bring me to the glider port by Black's. I park in the empty lot, grab a beach towel, and hop out. Throwing the towel into the bed of the truck, I hop in after it and lean back against the cab.

It's not a clear night. There are a few thin clouds in the sky. It was so good to speak with Jorge a couple weeks ago. It felt right. Like things were cleared up a bit between us.

"Hey man. You got a few?"

A slight breeze stirs up and I take that as a yes. Then I lean my head back against Esmerelda, the only reliable girl in my life besides Ma.

"There's this dude, Hien. I'm trying to help him. You know? And this guy Hop and I met up with a lawyer today. And he knows all about immigration stuff and asked questions I hadn't considered before. Like why did the guy leave his country? I know you and your Ma came here looking for work. I hadn't thought about people coming here to escape persecution from the government. I'm trying to imagine someone coming into St. Francis during mass and telling everyone to go home. That they couldn't worship anymore... I can't, and I'm all spazzed out worrying about Hien. So those are like real problems, right? Not like my petty, small-ass problems. But dude, those are bugging me too."

I sigh. "I got troubles. The femme kind. Yeah, I know. It's shit of me to complain, but you always knew what to do when it came to relationships. Remember Grace? The way-out-of-my-league crush? I thought my chances were pretty much zip, but sometimes she seemed into me. Still does. But I made a deal with her old man, and that makes her off-limits."

I fidget with the towel a few minutes, collecting my thoughts. "Her old man—he doesn't want anybody dating his little girl. Period. If I keep them away from her? He'll hook me up with the right law firm to push me on an early fast-track to law school. To meeting all the right people. Shit. Last week, he cc'd me on an email to Miguel Gutierrez.

Said we should meet for coffee. Hooked me up, even though he was pissed about Grace's accident. I don't like the way he makes me feel about things. Like he can ruin my career before it ever starts. Like he has the power to take my dreams from me before I even really get a chance to pursue them. That's messed up. But then he turns around and does me a favor. Says he knows I'll take better care of Grace."

I ball my hand into a fist and pound the bed of my truck a few times, until the side of my hands hurts. "It all sounds stupid when I tell you. Okay, I'll say out loud. I'm a tool, man. Why'd it take me so long to see it? Sometimes, doors slam shut. For a good reason. It's so obvious now. Her old man doesn't want anybody dating her, period. And if I ever date her, he'll have me blacklisted with every firm in town."

I pound my truck one more time. "That's it, dude. And you know what's crazy? There's a smart, beautiful girl at the office who actually seems into me. She asked *me* out. And there's no off-limits signs messing with my dreams if I date her. Sometimes when one door gets slammed shut, another one opens. Brianna's my open door."

twenty-three

Anxiety is the reaction to danger.
—Sigmund Freud

Ford squeezes my shoulder as he drops me off. "Come over to my place tonight and have dinner with my folks. Mom is making her famous chicken enchiladas. Deal?"

"Yum!" Ack—I frown. "I'll have to ask permission." Things at home are unpredictable again. I don't know if it's the cases my dad is working on, but blow-ups have been way more frequent in general and over the past week for sure. It makes me feel like I'm being sucked out in a riptide and I've forgotten how to paddle.

"Don't you ever think your folks are kind of uptight? You're always asking for permission. It's summertime. It seems like their panties must be in a perpetual wad."

I shrug. His hand hovers over the back of my jean shorts, ready to put *my* panties in a wad.

I shoot him a wicked grin. "Don't even think about it. I'm going commando."

His hand hovers there as his cheeks turn red. "Really?"

From the look on his face, I think he might have trouble concentrating on the way home. I give a little wave good-bye as he drives off.

Mom's car is parked under the laurel. I breathe a quiet sigh of relief. My odds of getting permission are decent as long as I make sure she realizes it's a friends-only dinner.

I search the front of the house—no mom. I call her name throughout the hallway—no mom. I peek in the office—no mom. My heart beats a little faster. Beads of sweat trickle at my hairline. Last resort, I knock on my parents' bedroom door—rap, rap, rap.

"Mom?"

Silence.

"Mom?"

I hear a rustling sound on the other side of the door. Jeez, could my heart pound any faster?

"Mom?"

The rustling sound moves closer to the door. I hear sniffling?

"Yes, Grace?"

Her voice sounds wobbly.

"Um, are you okay?" I tuck and untuck my hands in and out of my hoodie.

"I'm fine. What do you want?"

"Can I see you?" Tuck. Untuck. Tuck. Untuck.

"I'm busy right now. Do you need something?" Sniffle.

"Can I eat dinner at Ford's tonight?" I pull at the zipper.

"Yes, that's fine. Be home by eleven at the latest. Leave your father a note telling him where you are and that I said it was okay."

Deep breath. I shift back and forth like a waddling penguin. Tuck. Untuck. "Okay thanks. Are you sure you don't need anything?"

"No. I'm fine. Go to Ford's."

Holy shit. Something big must be going down. I sure as hell don't want to be here for the fireworks. "You sure you're okay?"

More sniffling. "Yes, honey. See you later."

I put my hand on the door and lean in. "Love you."

"Love you too, sweetie."

I speed down the hall, grab my backpack, and hurriedly scribble the note for my dad. I tape it to the refrigerator and rush toward my bike. This is one time when it's probably good I don't have a car—I'd be tempted to get on the freeway and keep driving. I grip the handlebars so tight my hands ache, but I can't loosen my grip. The muscles in my neck tense as I stress through the different scenarios of what could have upset my mom. I know the who—just not the how. Or the what. Or the why.

———

"Hey you," Ford calls out as he swings back and forth on his front porch. "I almost forgot to tell you—everybody at the office was talking about some major ass your dad kicked on one of his cases. He hasn't won it yet. But the key word is yet."

Distracted, I glance up at him as I pedal across the gravel drive. He's waiting for me, grinning. I wonder if he does that for Brittany. My smile falters as I greet him with a lame, "Hey."

I'm losing it. My ability to pretend everything is fine—when it's not. To pretend my dad is as cool as I wish he was …

Ford hops off the swing and bounds down the steps, meeting me halfway across the drive. He swoops in and takes my bike for me, leaning it against his house. He walks me inside. "*Mammi*, Dad—Grace is here." His voice resonates throughout the house.

Noise comes from the kitchen. The sound of a metal bowl hitting the floor clangs. It's followed by a string of unhappy Spanish and the sound of Mr. Watson's laughter.

By the time we rush into the kitchen, Mama Watson is laughing too. I gape in horror at their *saltillo*-tiled floor. The reddish-brown tiles are currently glazed in a light green *tomatillo* sauce.

Mr. Watson comes over and gives me a hug. "You came right in time for the show. Patricia is breaking into the art world with a bang. Some people paint on canvas; she paints on tile."

"Wow." The mess is mesmerizing.

"Well, Grace, I'd give you a hug too, but at the moment

we're divided by the Green Sea." She winks at me before holding a rag under running water. After giving it a squeeze she tosses it to Ford, who squats down to clean up the mess.

"Man, she makes a mess and I clean it. How's that for fair?" He pretends to grumble, but the dimple showing on his cheek gives him away.

"Eli, can you get out some more *tomatillo* sauce, sour cream, lime, and cilantro for me? Grace—would you mind setting the plates on the table?"

"Not at all." Glad as always to be included in the family, I grab red and yellow plates from the counter and begin setting them on the table, making sure each plate is centered in the front of the chair. Ford sweeps in behind me and places the silverware. I notice he actually knows which side the knife and fork go on and that he even sets the knife down so the blade faces inward. It's a little thing, but my heart flutters. I resist the urge to straighten the silverware. It's placed properly, if slightly askew. I smile. Kinda like Ford. Proper but not.

Mama Watson and Mr. Watson are in sync. He goes back and forth between her and the table, setting down serving dishes on hot pads and always returning for more. Meanwhile, Ford opens one of the glass cabinets. He pulls out four glasses, lines them up on the counter, then fills them up with water. I watch this seamless process in awe. Not one unkind word. No stress. Just quiet teamwork. It sounds silly, but it fascinates me.

I wonder if my mom is still crying. Whether or not she is okay. Who started the fight? Was it in person or over the phone? My stomach flops and I push all thoughts of home away.

After dinner, we head back to Ford's room. I feel Ford's eyes boring a hole in me as I say, "Your mom's enchiladas are amazing. You've been holding out on me."

Ford remains silent.

I stare at him. "Are you okay?"

He cocks his head to the side. "That's what I was wondering about you."

I curl my toes and press them into his rug as I lean back against a TV pillow. A heavy feeling sinks in my stomach. "What do you mean?"

He scoots closer to me. "You know what I mean. What's with you being upset so much and never giving an explanation? You're not as good at acting as you think you are. I could tell you were upset the second you walked up. It's driving me crazy. What's the deal?"

I stare at the floor. Tears trickle out. I hope my hair is hiding them. Ford tucks my hair behind my ears. Damn.

His arms envelope me and he presses his cheek against my wet one. It's a sacred moment, and neither one of us speaks.

Ford pulls back enough to look at me. "Why don't you trust me with whatever is upsetting you? At least give me a chance."

"I don't know. Things are too complicated—too messy." A little sigh shudders through me.

"What you mean is, what if I make things worse?" He massages my hands, relaxing them from the tight fists they were balled into.

I shrug my shoulders. "Sounds pretty crappy, huh?"

"No, just real. What if I promise on my honor not to make whatever it is worse?"

Considering my options, it seems like talking to Ford might be the best one. "Which includes not telling anyone else?"

Ford repeats, "Which includes not telling anyone else. Which I might add, is the business of trust. You confide in me and I don't share your secrets. And vice versa. Pretty nice concept—huh?"

"In theory, yes." My tears have dried up. "You swear?"

"A man's word is his bond." Ford grins.

I feel like I'm about to jump off the edge of a cliff. My pulse speeds up and my hands start sweating. "I'm serious. Swear?" I give him a pleading look. I have to know he's not just screwing around being silly.

"On a stack of Bibles. Pinky promise." His fingers interlock with mine. So yeah, he's keeping it light, trying to make me smile. But his eyes are serious and concerned, which is enough for me to feel safe.

"Okay, I'm gonna hold you to it." I scrutinize his face.

He gently takes my hands in his. "Jeez, Grace. Tell me already."

"Well, I don't even know where to start." I shift back and forth.

He scrunches in next to me against the TV pillow. "How about the weird vibes I get from your family?" he asks. "What's with that?"

My mouth dries up. I swallow as I absorb the question.

"Well … um, things aren't as happy as they seem. My folks don't exactly get along. And sometimes my dad can get carried away."

My cheeks burn. I squirm. What if Ford thinks I'm stupid? Or what if everybody's family is like mine? It's like part of me is freaking out about telling even this much, and another part of me is relieved.

"Like, overprotective? Carried away how?" Ford asks. His voice has a hard edge to it. He scoots closer to me.

"I don't know … he just does." I fidget with the frayed ends of my jeans and keep my eyes focused on the rug. I'm afraid to see the expression on Ford's face.

"Like he's a prosecutor in a courtroom?"

"No. Never mind. Life isn't all courtroom drama. Forget I said anything."

Ford bristles. "I'm trying to figure out what you mean. Carried away … "

I'm exhausted. "Why do we have to talk about this right now? About my crap? What about yours? Like, tell me more about Brittany?" The momentary escape is slipping through my fingers with every word I speak.

Ford gives me a puzzled look before scooting away from me. A long silence stretches on into eternity, like he can't decide whether to push or be okay with what I've said. I hold my breath.

He says, "I don't know who Brittany is … why don't you tell me what you're talking about?"

The fact that he's playing stupid irritates me. Like I want to put up with that kind of crap. What kind of friend is he anyway? I stand up and put my hands on my hips. "The girl. The hot one that you're coaching."

He forces a smile. "Brianna? She's not training. I just gave her a beginner's lesson that one day. She's a girl from work. What's up?"

Even though we're not together, it feels like he's cheating on me. I swallow. It's like I'm playing chicken with heartache. "Nothing. It's just … she seemed like a nice girl. Pretty. You should … you know. Go for her."

Ford crosses his arms. "You know, Grace, I don't need your approval or permission to date anyone. And Brianna and I have gone on a date—bowling. But … thanks for the advice." He stares me down, a puzzled look on his face.

I steel my insides, wondering what in the world is wrong with me. Why do I keep pushing him away?

twenty-four

advice: *recommendation regarding
a decision or course of conduct
—www.merriam-webster.com*

You should... you know. Go for her.

Those seven words, combined with the completely un-readable look on Grace's face as she said them, was on repeat all night long. And every time I process that stupid conver-sation, I get more irritated. What makes her think I need her permission? And what is *she* doing? Rubbing things in my face? It almost feels like she's just throwing shit at the fan to watch it fly because she doesn't want to deal with her own crap.

I blink open my eyes wider, trying to wake up as I gulp coffee on my way to work. I'm not used to losing sleep, period. And having my eyes feel like they're recovering from an acid wash doesn't endear Grace to me further.

I rush up the stairs and enter the office at the same time as Mr. Parker.

His voice booms, "Morning, Ford. Walk with me."

"Yes sir." My left eye twitches as I follow him like a prisoner to the guillotine, my mind racing. He doesn't say anything. Instead, we walk down the hall silently, which is more ominous to me than the eerie calm before a storm.

He opens his office door, makes two giant strides toward his desk, plops down, and motions for me to take a seat.

I pull back the leather chair and sit on the edge, ready to bolt.

He leans back in his chair like he has all the time in the world, which can't be true. He's still up to his eyeballs in that Thompson case. "How do you think the summer is going?"

"Pretty good, sir."

"You keeping the guys away from my little girl?"

"Doing my best, sir." Forget the fact that I'm burning up mad and not planning on talking to Grace for a few days at least.

He sits up straight. "Is that good enough?"

"I think so. She's not dating anyone."

He puts a fist down gently on the desk. "That works." Then he looks me straight in the eyes. "You're a pretty smooth guy. I hear you have a side project going."

What is he talking about? Nothing's happened with Grace. Brianna? I'm kerflummoxed, so I play it safe and wait for him to keep talking.

"Hollingsworth?"

Worried about Hien's help blowing up, I scoot to the very edge of the seat. "Is that a problem, sir?"

He laughs. "What Hollingsworth does on his time is his business. He's got a long way to make senior partner, and one pro bono isn't going to change that. Just make sure when you're here that you're working on the things you've been asked to do. Anything that belongs after hours belongs after hours. Are we square on that, son?"

Doing my best to keep a poker face, I say, "Yes sir. Is that all?"

He stands up, smoothly guiding me to the door with his body cues. "That's all."

I exit his office fuming, but remind myself he's helped a lot of people. A lot of my people.

———

Engine parts are scattered in neat piles across our garage floor. Everything has an order to it. There's a reason for the way it's laid out—it makes it easier when Dad needs that part later. His methodical approach to rebuilding engines extends into everyday life. He doesn't say a lot, but when he does, I listen. The kickass thing about my dad is that his words match his actions.

He's rehabbing an old Jag. V12 engine, 575 horsepower. A type-E Roadster convertible. Sleek lines. The kind of car that gives every red-blooded teenage guy a hard-on. The car is sick. In the best way.

Dad holds out his hand; I pass him a socket wrench. He

leans back over the engine, finagling his hands in tight spaces because he's a pro. Someday, I want to know engines as well as my dad. There's something about being able to fix something with your own hands, a feeling of complete satisfaction.

Mr. Parker was a total douche this morning. The conversation with Grace last night, the way she was so upset. And the words "carried away" are etched in my brain as sure as the memory of Kahuna Pete carrying her limp body onto the beach. It's hard to know what she meant by all that. How much she's not saying. Yeah, her old man can certainly let people have it in court. Every word is calculated to his advantage, building his case. And then there was that morning in his office after Grace's accident, when he had fun playing cat and mouse. Testing me. Is that what's she's talking about? Does he push her into verbal corners? Or is it more? He can be a hardass, but he's also done a lot of good for a lot of people.

Sometimes I don't understand what Grace does or says. She doesn't want to date, but we have all these little moments where I think she wants more or she seems jealous. Then there's the whole Brittany/Brianna thing. She was all worked up, like she was itching for a fight. Then she told me to date Brianna? I don't get it.

"Dad?" I ask. "How'd you know Ma was the one?"

Dad pops up from the car, knocking his head on the hood. He flinches and grabs the back of his head, grinning sheepishly. "What's that?"

I shake hair out of my eyes. "You know. How do you know when to make the move to date someone?"

He steps back and sits on a stool, grinning. "Is it Grace?"

Frustrated, I shake my head no.

He gets this concerned look. "What happened, son?"

His "son" reminds me of Mr. Parker's "son," and that how someone says a word can make all the difference. I walk over to his toolbox and start messing with a socket wrench, winding it around.

He says, "Did you two fight last night?"

I say, "Kind of. But that's not the problem."

"Then what is?"

I hesitate before I say it out loud. To Dad. Admit rejection. End it fast. "She doesn't want me. She's into surfing. That's it."

Dad says, "Well, maybe she needs time."

Nope. He doesn't get it. Shit. I hate saying it. "Dad, I pretty much asked her out at the beginning of the summer and she shot me down. Grace and I are nothing more than good friends. Really." Flashes of the moments when Grace and I were doing something together and I felt sparks drive me crazy. Like the time at the Point when I swear she was going to kiss me. But that's crazy wishful thinking. With Grace, I feel like I doubt everything. I don't have any gut instincts anymore and I'm sick to my stomach. Angry. I need to burn off some energy.

He grabs a rag and scrubs at grease on his arms. "Then who's the girl?"

"Brianna from work."

"The one you took surfing?"

I grin. She was so clueless and fun. It's one of the first

times in a while where I hung out at the beach without worrying about saying the wrong thing to Grace or worrying about some tool hitting on her. The beach just isn't as stellar this summer. It's like Grace and her dad have sucked a lot of the fun out of it. "Yeah."

He smiles. "She likes you, huh?"

I start feeling a little better. "She asked me out too."

"You like her?"

After a split second, I say, "Yeah. I think so."

Dad throws the towel at me. I dodge, blocking it with my arm. He grins and says, "Then go for it."

I nod. "Yeah. I think I will."

But I can't get Grace out of my head. Our conversation last night. Her vague explanations. It nags at me, like my little cousin Carlos who won't quit pulling on your pants until he gets what he wants.

I ask Dad, "What do you do when somebody seems like they're in trouble? Kind of serious... but you don't know what it is."

Dad angles his body under the hood and grunts. Then he says, "Well, I don't see there's much you can do to help someone if you don't know what kind of help they need." Then he pops out from under the hood, sets down the wrench, and wipes his hands on his jeans. "Son, you'll run across situations in life where you don't know all the angles. That's when you need to trust your gut and read between the lines."

Then he gives me the Dad-pat-on-the-shoulder move. One of those *I imparted wisdom son* looks with a whack on the shoulder to show he cares. Which is great... 'cause he does. But what do you do when you don't know what lines to read between?

twenty-five

*In the end, who among us does
not choose to be a little less
right to be a little less lonely.*
—Robert Brault

Thanks to it being a rainy day, my weekly run with Mom is a no go. I look out the kitchen window and sigh. I needed to burn off some steam this afternoon.

Mom says, "Bummed about the run?"

"I was looking forward to getting out." I was looking forward to time with her, to hanging out without getting into a catfight.

She pads across the floor and stands by me, watching the rain drill everything in its path. "Well, just because we can't run doesn't mean we can't get out for an hour. We've got options."

"What?"

She puts her arm around my waist in a hug. "Did you

ever stop to think your dear old mom has a pretty nice vehicle, that works? Let's go to the Chocolat Café. We can splurge on French pastries."

Whoa. Splurge on extra calories? Empty ones? Wow. Mom must have had a super shitty week. Although the Chocolat Café isn't what I had in mind, it's a fun back-up plan. Maybe we can talk … about whatever happened a couple of nights ago.

"Okay then." Mom pats my knee. "We'll leave in fifteen minutes. I'll touch up my makeup and change tops."

"All righty."

"Grace?"

"Hmm."

"You're gonna do a few touch-ups too, right? Just a little lip gloss and maybe change into a nicer shirt?"

Never good enough.

"Sure, Mom. I'll change."

––––––––––

Mom is totally anti-chain stores. She's all about helping Mom and Pop shops—until it comes to groceries or gas stations. I guess everyone draws a line somewhere.

She sips her café au lait, fingers laced around it. Then she takes a dainty bite of a chocolate croissant.

I slurp some whipped cream melting into my white chocolate mocha and accidentally suck up more mocha than cream. The roof of my mouth is officially burned. A little flap of skin hangs down, a reminder of my stupidity. Yay.

"So, what's going on with you and Ford lately?"

I wipe at the cream on my upper lip, a tactical maneuver to hide my surprise.

Mom adds, "Didn't you go over to his house for dinner the other night?" We haven't really spoken since the night she was a wreck.

"Nothing's going on," I say. "And the girl he's dating isn't named Brittany. It's Brianna." Saying her name is like biting into a lemon. "I don't have time to mess with a relationship. Besides, Ford's been a real tool lately."

She nods her head, with a kind of knowing look like she knew he would disappoint me all along, which totally burns me. He's not that kind of guy. Usually. "You're absolutely right, sweetheart. Ford seemed like a nice guy. They all do at first, though…" Her voice trails off and she stares at a 1950s beach advertisement. There's a young couple in swimsuits looking like they've found nirvana. She looks wistful; I feel sad for her. "Your father was quite the surfer when we first met."

"Mom…if you want to talk about things…" My voice trails off and I realize how lame I must sound.

She snaps to and paints a smile on her face. Her bright chipper reaction amazes me. It's like she doesn't recognize the fact we live in the same house. "Things? There's nothing to discuss."

She stands up, café au lait in hand, and motions me to follow her to the car. Great. After a nice afternoon, I screw things up.

Once inside the car, Mom doesn't start the engine. She sighs and tears well up at the corner of her eyes.

"What's wrong?"

Mom pauses.

"Is it Dad?"

Mom says, "You know I love your father. I really do, but sometimes it's ... well, it's just hard."

My mouth opens a little bit. I burst out, "What happened the other night? Why were you so upset?"

Her fingers grip the steering wheel. "Nothing happened. Your father and I got into an argument."

"About what?" I kick off my flip-flops, pull my knees to my chest, and turn toward her. This is not an everyday conversation.

"About money, about relationships, about his temper."

"Way to go, Mom!"

Apparently my encouragement isn't welcome. She takes the one wild, lone strand of hair and tucks it carefully back into place. "Do you think I haven't had these conversations before? Do you think we haven't argued about these topics? We do all the time, and it always ends the same—with me hurt and nothing gained."

Everything has been piling up like dirty laundry I can't ignore. It's driving me crazy. If she doesn't leave, then I'm stuck here too. I push. "Then why stay?"

She throws back her head and laughs a dry, eerie laugh. "Get real. Like I've told you before, at my age I'm not looking for change or planning on announcing my failures to the world. I said my vows and I meant them—for better or worse." She white-knuckles the steering wheel, puts on her fake happy, and pulls out of the parking space with perfect control.

Are you kidding me? "What about his vows? 'To love and to cherish?'"

"Don't start."

"Don't start? What? Were his vows different than yours?"

"Grace—"

"Or maybe his didn't count?"

She slams on the brake. The seat belt locks me in and jolts me back.

"Don't talk to me like that, young lady. You have no idea what I put up with so you can have a father."

I adjust the seat belt. "Hello? I live with him too."

"Do you know how many girls I've seen in court that were selling themselves on the street or doing drugs? Do you know what their defense was? No father figure. The way I see it, you're pretty damn lucky. And you're sure as hell doing well in school and life…someday you'll thank me. Someday, you'll see."

twenty-six

console: *to alleviate the grief, sense of loss, or trouble of*
—www.merriam-webster.com

It's been five days since Grace and I had our spat. Her not explaining whatever is making her so upset, and me throwing Brianna in her face. I shouldn't have done that. It's irritating— I can't fix a problem if I don't know what it is. Dodging Mr. Parker at the office recently has taken a Herculean effort. It's not all about me anymore; Hien could get screwed if I mess up. And I'm bummed and stressed about everything. I pick up my cell and text Brianna.

My fingers hover over the keyboard before writing,

Wanna go out tonight?

Ping. Crap. Fast response. I click on View.

Like on a second date? :)

I hesitate, then write,

You know it.

What time? Seven?

See you then.

I shove my phone in my pocket, annoyed that Grace has taken up such permanent residence in my mind. I deserve somebody like Brianna. Somebody who wants me. Period. Why the heck has it taken me so long to get that? Just realizing it makes me feel stronger, ready to conquer the world. Okay fine, truth is, I'm ecstatic to have an awesome date.

———————

I knock on the door of Brianna's condo, wondering if her folks are there and what kind of people they are...

A lady answers the door. She's pretty. A slightly larger, older version of Brianna. She smiles at me. "You must be Ford. I'm Nadine. It's nice to meet you."

We shake. I say, "It's nice to meet you too."

Brianna zips in next to her mom. "Oh no you don't." She grins. "If I don't get you out of here now, Mom will have you on the couch flipping through baby pictures of me in the buff."

I glance at her mom and kind of smile-shrug, to make sure she's cool with us heading out.

She nods her approval. "You two have fun. Be back by midnight!"

I say, "Yes ma'am."

Once we're in the truck, I check Brianna out as she sits next to me, looking gorgeous. She's wearing a dark brown top that hugs her chest and then hangs loose. Her jeans hug her thighs. Her long silver earrings dance with her braids as she tilts her head, smiling. She's really beautiful, but even better than that? She's smart and she shoots straight. She knows what she wants and I know where I stand with her.

I start Esmerelda and check Brianna out one more time. "All right, ma'am. Let's roll."

After we have dinner at a casual sushi bar, I decide to go the romantic route. Once we're back in the truck, I ask, "You want to hang out at Black's?"

"Is that a club?"

I laugh. "No, it's a beach."

She says, "I guess."

I crank up the engine. "You ever hung out at the beach at night?"

"No."

I grin, excited to share it with her. "It's magic."

She scoots over to the middle of the bench seat and buckles up, resting her leg against mine. I turn on some Ben Harper and off we go.

When I pull into the parking lot at the glider port, it's virtually empty. Except for a few lone vehicles.

The sunset is almost complete. "Crap. We better hurry."

I rush out of the truck while Brianna puts on lip gloss. Then she exits with finesse, no struggle. "Wow," I say. "I think Esmerelda likes you."

She pats the truck's side. "Of course she does."

I shut the door behind her. "The view from the cliffs is sweet."

"It's really pretty out here," she says.

We head to my favorite patch of grass and sit. Brianna shifts uncomfortably.

"What's wrong?" I ask.

She makes a face. "This isn't exactly the right kind of outfit for sitting in dirt."

I pat my lap. "I'll protect you."

She grins. "Well, okay." She settles into my lap.

I shift, trying to make sure she's comfortable. I peek around her, trying to focus on the sunset. It's a red sliver on the ocean.

"You're a really cool guy ... you know, what you and Hop are doing for his friend. It's huge."

Embarrassed to take credit for something I wish I could do more about, I say, "It's Hollingsworth who's going to kick ass. We just got them connected. But someday…"

"Someday you're going to be the one kicking courtroom ass." Then Brianna turns and whispers in my ear, "It's a great view."

I happily agree, looking at the red streak glowing across the sky. "Yeah, it is."

She nuzzles me. "No. You."

My face feels hot.

She places her hands on my cheeks. "You're so cute. Acting all embarrassed."

"Look who's talking."

She leans forward, her minty breath warm on my face. I close my eyes and give in. Heaven. I glance at her, heart pounding. I lean in to kiss her, and she meets me halfway. My pulse pumps like a jackhammer. I kiss her soft and slow, crumbling. Her earrings jingle. I'm trying to rein things in. Use self control. She's a sweet girl. I haven't really even made out with anyone before. I've been holding out for Grace.

And Grace. Crap. She doesn't belong here.

I focus on Brianna and lean in for another kiss.

twenty-seven

*It is an equal failing to trust
everybody and to trust nobody.*
—Thomas Fuller

This past week has been tense. Mom's been working late hours. My normally clean room looks like someone else lives in it; it's as disheveled as I feel. Ford and I haven't made up yet, and I know our argument wasn't big enough for this. It seems like every time I call or text, he's busy with work stuff or hanging out with his new friends. I don't understand why he's acting like this. *Hello*, the surf comp is in four days and I still haven't nailed the 360.

Damien should be here any minute. He's been a lifesaver. If it weren't for him, I don't know how I would have made it to the beach so much this week. I snag my cell, throw my duffel over my shoulder, and run for the garage. I can't stand being late. The screwier things get, the earlier I like to be.

Early is on time. On time is barely making it. And being late equals major stress.

Bam. I crash into Dad in the hallway. What the crap?

"Sorry, Dad. I didn't realize anyone was home. I thought you were at the office this morning."

He raises the back of his hand and then stops. I flinch. He grits his teeth. "That doesn't mean you run around wild, crashing into things. You're going to scrape the paint on our walls. Show some respect."

The last thing I need is Damien knocking on our front door and hearing Dad yell at me or worse. "Sorry, Dad. I won't run in the hall anymore. Damien should be here any minute and I didn't want to make him wait."

"Get the hell out on the porch and wait for him, then. I've got a case to work on. Are your chores finished?"

Is he nuts? It's seven in the morning. In the summer. Who has their chores finished?

I do the only thing I can do—lie. "I started earlier this morning. I'm almost finished. I'll have them done by the time you get home this evening."

I bank on the fact that he needs to get to work and I'm about to leave. Good God, I'm tired of lying. It feels like my entire life is one big lie. Lie to everyone about what a wonderful family I have. Lie to dad about chores. Lie to mom about surfing and college and how I feel about Ford. Lie to Ford about not wanting to date him. That's the one that makes me feel the worst.

He snarls, "Make sure you do."

"Yes sir."

Our zen-sounding door bell chimes. How ironic. I feel anything but calm.

"That's probably Damien. I should answer the door." I wait for Dad's approval, dying that I'm now late.

"Get moving, then. I'll see you tonight."

"Okay, thanks. Bye Daddy." I speed-walk to the front door and try to shake off the adrenaline rushing through me. It's all good. I'm going surfing. All I need to do is work on surf skills and keep up with my chores. Then everything will fall into place.

I open the door with my best fake smile. "Hey. Sorry to make you wait."

Damien takes my duffel bag. "No worries."

"Thanks." I punch in the code for the garage and duck underneath the door while it's still rising. I snag my board and hurry out. Escape. That's what I want. That's where I'm headed. I close the door. Damien takes the board.

And then I deflate. "Crap."

"What?"

"I forgot to fill the jugs with hot water," I say, tucking my hands in and out of my sleeves. Damien and I have been rinsing off with fresh warm water after our surf sessions. It's a little thing, but it feels so good.

"Chillax, girl. I'll get your board strapped in, no rush."

This is so not the day to go back inside and risk another run-in. But what am I supposed to say to Damien? *We don't have hot water? I'm extra-scared of Dad this morning?* Yeah, right. I bite my lip and trudge back to the house. As I step through the front door, I hear cursing come from my bedroom. Shit.

Forget it. Just go, go, go. I rush to the pantry to grab some empty water jugs and fill them up as quickly as possible. Thank God we have an instant hot water tap. I'm working on jug number two when I hear heavy footsteps closing in on me. I'll play dumb.

"Oh hey, Daddy. I forgot the hot water jugs. I'll be out of your way in just a minute." I glance backward to see dirty laundry in his hands.

"'Almost finished,' huh? I'd sure as hell hate to see what 'haven't even started' looks like."

"It's really not that much. It looks worse than it is." My pulse quickens and I consider bailing—leaving the jugs on the counter, running and never coming back. Instead I pop the lid onto the jug. Damien will think I'm crazy if I walk out without these things full, and I don't want to explain any more than I want to face Dad right now.

He slams the laundry on the table. "Then you'll have no problem showing me what spotless looks like tomorrow morning."

I cringe. "Yes sir."

He flings his arm in the air and shoos me toward the door. "Well, what's wrong with you? You're making him wait."

"Yes sir." I grab the jugs and scramble for the door, but not before getting a hard backhand on my rear on the way out. I guess that's the only place he can be sure Damien won't see, if it leaves a mark.

Tears smart my eyes. I won't cry; he won't win.

I jerk the Jeep door open and shove the water jugs onto the floorboard, then slam the door, blinking back tears and hoping Damien isn't looking at me.

"Easy there. I waxed her yesterday. Everything okay?"

"Everything's fine." My voice comes out raspy, but if I try to clear my throat it will just make it more obvious. "I guess I'm in a rush."

Silence lingers for a minute. "The waves'll be there. What's with the hurry?"

I swallow hard, trying to clear my throat. "Too much."

Damien turns to me. "Want to talk about it?"

Please God, start the engine already. We need to go. I need to get out of here.

"Not really," I say, kicking off my turquoise flip-flops and drawing my knees to my chest.

He eyes Dad's car in the driveway and nods like he understands. "It's cool. If you change your mind . . . I'm here."

If only he knew. I don't answer. I stare out the window. I screwed things up with Ford. Our relationship is ruined. He's got new peeps. I don't want to do the same with Damien. I mumble, "It's just the fact that my parents kind of have unrealistic expectations. You know? And sometimes my dad gets fired up when he's pissed."

He drives down the street away from our house, and with every foot between me and my dad, I feel a nervous energy pulsing through me. I'm unsure as to whether I'm going to laugh or cry or scream.

Damien stays quiet as we exit the neighborhood and I feel dumb for saying anything. I know better than that.

Nobody ever wants the truth, not even close to it. It was a moment of weakness. I lost control of my emotions.

Once Damien gets on the highway he says, "Does that mean what I think it means? Like, he's physical toward you?"

I squirm like an ant under a magnifying glass in the hot sun, my pulse quickening as a lump the size of a brick fills up my throat. I'm miserable; scraping Grimace Rock was a picnic compared to the humiliation weighing on me like a two-ton elephant.

He runs his right hand back over his dreads and then places it back on the wheel. He sucks in a big breath of air, starts to say something, and then stops.

I'm dying. This is why I never say anything. It's not like anyone can do anything.

He blows air out his mouth and exits the freeway, where he flies across the frontage and whips into the first parking lot he can turn into. He parks and turns to me, intense. I'm wishing I could disappear.

He says, "You know you don't have to put up with that. Right? It's total crap. You know that. C'mon, you're so freaking smart. Why the hell are you still there?"

And while I agree it's crap, I'm angry. At my parents, my situation, at not knowing who to trust, at humiliating myself, at Damien's judgment of me.

Bitter, I vomit words and random thoughts. "Oh, like it's all that easy. Sure, I'll just move out of my house. To where? With who? And are they going to love me? Like really love me? And why would they? And what about college? Are they going to pay for my education?"

Damien's eyes grow big and he places his hand on the console between us. "I'm sorry. I know it's complicated."

I turn my head. "It's more than that, and it's not out of control. I mean ... I can handle it. I got one more year, and then they pay for my college and I'm out of there. For good."

Damien's hands shake a little and his voice comes out real quiet. "But at what price?"

"Can we just go? More than anything, I need to surf today. Please? And don't say anything. Nobody knows."

"Not even Ford?"

I half whisper, "Not even Ford."

———————

I. Did. It. I surfed the freaking Point and lived to tell. No scratches.

After that conversation with Damien, I needed to blow off steam. I surfed my ass off today. I avoided the rocks and I surfed the Point. All day. Now I'm laid out on the sand like a wet noodle. Ecstatic. Exhausted. I can't wait to tell Ford. But I don't want to go home for anything. Who knows when Mom will be home? And I don't want another run-in with Dad.

Damien sits beside me looking like a Billabong surfer ad.

I stretch out. "Ugh. I don't want this day to end."

"Then don't let it. Let's live on the edge."

"How?" I sit up and grin mischievously at Damien, grateful he let things drop. Glad we had a good day. As far as I'm concerned, I'm going to act like I never said anything and it looks like Damien will do the same.

He pulls back a little, tries to hide his surprise. He taps his chin with his pointer finger like he's thinking hard. Then he smirks. He snaps his fingers and shrugs. "Guess we'll have to go shopping ... on my old man's card."

I laugh, half shocked and completely amused. "No way."

He stands up and puts my bag over his shoulder like a girl wears a purse. "Yes way. Girl, I can be cray-cray. C'mon," he wheedles.

He's so hot, standing there acting stupid. Wearing my bag. So tempting. For a split second I close my eyes. Then I give in. "I'm in. What's that saying?" I twist around to pop my back. Got it. "Sometimes it's better to ask forgiveness than permission."

He holds an arm out. We link elbows. Damien cracks me up. He's a blast.

We get out of the Jeep in front of Goodwill and I walk on the lawn instead of the sidewalk. Such a stupid little thing, but I feel like such a rebel. Ford would be so proud. Crap. I've got to get him out of my head. Today I'm having fun—with Damien. Be gone, Ford Watson.

twenty-eight

Rubbernecker: *a person who slows their vehicle down to look at a wreck they're driving past*

Hanging out on my front porch after a great day at the office. Flip-flopping it. Playing guitar. My kind of late afternoon.

My cell dings. I check the message. It's Grace. I feel kind of bad. We haven't really hung out since we argued about Brianna. And I haven't been blowing her off on purpose. Just kind of got caught up hanging out with Brianna. And then the guys had an epic poker tournament. After that much time with Little Hien, I feel like I could host *MTV Cribs* or something.

> Can we talk?

Wow. I wonder what made her make the first move.

> Yeah. Where?

Your place?

C'mon over.

See you soon.

It's so funny, Grace's text. Even her text speak is proper. Brianna would have written CU soon. And added a smiley face. Because she's cute like that.

Grace can be all business. She can be a lot of fun, too. Not surfing with Grace the past week was weird. Things haven't felt right. Like the world isn't spinning on the right axis. I heard she surfed all week with Damien. He's such a butt-munch.

Grace speeds into the driveway, parks her bike, and bounds up the steps with the biggest smile I've seen on her face in weeks.

I strum a chord. "Hey, *Mamacita*." I set the guitar down and give her a big hug. Strangely self-conscious, I say, "Um, I need to snag a shirt." I head into the house with Grace trailing behind, grab a shirt off the top of the laundry basket, and yank it on, enjoying this Grace. "You're in a hella good mood. What's up?"

She squeals, "I surfed the Point!"

I frown. "What?"

She squeals again. "Yeah. I surfed the Point!" Then she twirls around. "And I lived to tell."

That's crazy. "What the hell? You went without me?"

She jerks to a stop. "What do you mean?"

"Excuse me, but last time we surfed there, you almost died."

She glares daggers. "Wow. I thought you'd be happy for me."

I throw my hands in the air. "I thought we had a thing. I'm supposed to be your coach. Who watched out for you?"

She cocks her head, places her hand on her hips. "Newsflash—last time I checked, a coach goes with you to the beach. Some coach you've been. Since you've been MIA, Damien's surfed with me. The comp is this week. What did you expect? Besides, I needed to go back there. Face my fears and all."

She's right. Sort of. But Damien? He's a dillweed. Stab me in the heart. "Oh, so Damien took care of you like I would have, huh? Besides, the only reason I haven't taken you there is because your dad specifically told me not to—"

"Well, Damien took care of me. It's fine."

Something about the way she said that really sets me off. "Oh, yeah, I bet he did. Did he watch out for you? Make sure you were safe?"

Grace narrows her eyes. "Oh. Like you, that day at the Point?"

Wow. Going in for the kill. "What are you talking about?"

She says, "Oh, wait, maybe I'm confused. I thought Kahuna Pete pulled me out. Where were you? Oh, wait, that's right, you showed up right afterward to 'claim' me as your girl."

Air quotes are the last straw. I say, "I can't believe you went there. Is that what you think of me?" Palm to the face. "I've been reduced to a cheap cliché. You say we're friends, but you sure as hell don't act like it. See ya. Don't let the door hit your ass on the way out." I look up to watch her go. Like a rubbernecker on the highway. We're a freaking train wreck.

She scowls, her eyes narrowed and forehead scrunched up.

I scowl back, but then I waver. I shove my hands in my pockets.

She says, "Fine. I'm outtie," and heads toward the door.

I run after her, like the idiot I can't help being. "Grace, wait."

She throws a hand up in the air and doesn't even look at me. She huffs out of the houses and marches toward her bike. This is crazy. "*Please*," I say.

And she keeps walking. Away. From me.

And me? I trail after like a stray dog wanting a home. "C'mon, Grace. At least let me give you a ride."

Nothing. A shove of her flip-flop on a pedal and she's off. Gone.

I'm not letting her do this to me. Treat me like a cheap throw-away. I yell after her, "Oh yeah? If you're gonna act like a cold-hearted B, then good luck at the comp. You're on your own."

twenty-nine

*Courage, sacrifice, determination,
commitment, toughness, heart, talent,
guts. That's what little girls are made
of; the heck with sugar and spice.*
—Bethany Hamilton

Today is a welcome diversion even if it means surfing by myself. The comp's tomorrow and I feel so screwed up, but Ford or no Ford, I've gotta surf. Mom even let me borrow the Jeep, which is a total first … she didn't even grill me about why I needed transportation. Whatever is going on with her, she's too stressed to care about what I'm doing. Of course, she'd have a conniption if she knew I was surfing by myself. I didn't want a ride from Damien, even though he would have been cool with it. Part of me is nervous about surfing with him after our day at the Point. I'm worried about what he'll say and if he'll bring up my dad.

Anyway, all my energy needs to be focused on the comp.

On controlling myself and my moves. On figuring out the 360. On my own. On wowing the UCSD surf coach. On not losing the only thing I have in life, surfing my favorite beaches.

So I drive into Black's with music blaring, feeling the need to surf until I burn off some stress. I wriggle into my wetsuit, unload my board, sling a backpack over my shoulder, and head for the beach.

Waves are breaking right and a handful of surfers are out. I didn't see Esmerelda in the parking lot, not that I expected Ford to be here. My eyes are raw from crying for the past few days. They feel like someone took Coke bottles, smashed them up to tiny pieces, and taped them to my eyelids. Salt water is going to suck today. The thing that I never wanted to happen—losing my best friend—happened. I lost him to the girl I told him to date. 'Cause I'm an idiot.

I wax and comb my board, watching guys rip moves I need to perfect. The last thing I need is to be a joke at the comp. This is my chance. All I need is to maintain better control of my life. I slipped up. Let emotions get in the way. Well, no stupid boy is going to get in the way of my dreams. Neither are my parents. I will do it. I will kick ass. I have to win. That's all I have.

After a quick glance around, I shove my backpack in an inconspicuous spot half-covered by a rock and schlep toward the ocean. A gust of cold wind reminds me that I haven't zipped up my wetsuit, and why would I? Ford does that for me. But I don't need him. I can zip my own freaking wetsuit. It's not like it's that big of a deal. Wetsuits have long tags attached to the end of the zipper so the user doesn't need anyone else. Damn it, why did Ford and I have to fight the week before the comp?

As I finish fixing my wetsuit and lean over to snag my board, a little strand of hair at the nape of my neck rips out. Grr. Stupid Ford. Stupid zipper. Stupid me.

I huff out to thigh-deep water before jumping on my board and paddling out. I don't even wince at cold water attacking me in all the wrong places.

I make it out to the breakers, winded. I hope I didn't use all my pissed-off energy up getting here and then not be able to catch anything. There are five other surfers out here, but they're all guys. Surfing without Ford or Damien makes me a smidge nervous. Nobody has my back, but maybe that's been true all along. The one person I thought I could count on ... well, forget it.

Some college-age jerkwad with his roots showing says, "You paddled out to play with the big dogs, so don't expect any free rides. Unless you want one in the backseat of my Hummer."

I flip him off. "Trying to impress me with your gas guzzler? No thanks, Assclown. The only thing I plan on riding? Waves that you want."

Another dude in a deep blue wetsuit says, "Nice one. Don't pay attention to Assclown. He's all bark and no action ... anywhere. And since he gave you such a warm welcome, take your pick off the next set."

"Thanks." If Ford were here, Assclown wouldn't have given me more than a second glance.

Assclown doesn't argue about me picking out my wave. He grumbles, "This ain't no tea party."

I ignore him. When the next set comes in, I paddle hard for the first wave, almost too hard. I ease up and catch the sweet spot. My mind goes blank to anything but this. I *love* it—the sheer joy that wells up inside me as I carve switch-backs up and down the wave. As the time to exit or ride it in approaches, I'm pumped and decide to end with a 360. But I hesitate near the end of the spin, and down I go. Water collides with my face and I reach for my nose to keep water from rushing up it. Ugh—that split second where I don't have control? I can't stand it, and it bites me in the ass every time. I have three days and I still haven't perfected a move that says *I'm here to win.*

Of course, oh yay. Here comes Ford, paddling right toward me. Am I supposed to pretend we didn't have an argument? There's no way I'm apologizing. The words "cold-hearted B" are freshly etched in my mind. Those three little words pretty much add all the fuel I need to continue my fire. The only other person who's ever called me a bitch was my dad. Using the first letter doesn't soften the blow. It gives me something to use when I need ammo to win my next argument with Ford.

I pooch my lips, give a quick raise of the eyebrows, and pull my mouth up to one side. Whatev. I'm here to surf, not play footsies. Everything I've worked for is going down tomorrow and the last thing I need is more crap from Ford or my parents. I still haven't completed more than one page of one Ivy League essay app yet. Not gonna happen. I categorically refuse to go to college out of state. I just have to figure out the right timing to break it to them, when they're ready to be rational and listen.

Ford parks a shiny new longboard a couple of feet from me and doesn't even say hey.

Two can play that game. I ignore his new toy, give him the slightest nod, and then turn away to focus on the next set coming in. He follows suit. Thank God there's actually one rushing at us. It's a competition now. I pop back around and lie down on my board, ready to paddle with everything I've got. When it's a couple of feet behind me, I dig deep into the water with forward strokes, feeding off my anger, and propel myself forward as hard as possible. It's a paddle battle, but I'm in a better position to catch the sweet spot. I grin as my board gets pulled up into the top of the wave and watch Ford float over the top.

I laugh, enjoying the blast of ocean on my heels, as I make my bottom turn and pull a couple of cutbacks. I zip across the face, gain momentum, and then catch a little air off the backside before making my exit. A little spray, a little show to let Ford know I can do fine on my own.

I paddle past him as he carves on his own ride. He pulls a floater and then does some fancy cross-stepping before managing to hang five like it's a breeze. Showoff. I pull my board up on the outside of Assclown's group. Not close enough to have to fight them for waves, but just on the outskirts where I can kind of pretend I'm with them … if I want.

Ford paddles over and settles in a few feet away from me. He says, "Nice ride."

I give him a curt "Thanks."

Silence. Tension.

I decide to make the next move. "So, new board?"

Ford nods. "I've been eyeing this for a while. Jake at the surf shop let me borrow it for the day. I'll probably buy it. It has a good feel." He hesitates. "Wanna try it?"

That's the ultimate peace offering, but I won't let myself forget our argument. He didn't even call to apologize. Besides, I have the comp to train for, which means I should stick to my board. I say, "Nah. Thanks anyway."

His face falls. So I add, "I'll take a rain check for after you buy it. Gotta stick with mine until the comp tomorrow."

His forearms flex as he grips the board, and my eyes travel up his torso. My cheeks burn, embarrassed to be wishing I could see his washboard abs.

He says, "Yeah, right. How's your afternoon been?"

My eyes take in his dimple and lock with his eyes; I realize he totally knows I just checked him out. I blush and look away, wondering if Brianna checks him out like that and if she realizes all the other things to love about him—like how smart or funny he is and how thoughtful he can be.

He kicks his board over to mine, the distance between us fluctuating with the gentle slopes of the ocean. I breathe in and remind myself that I should be mad, that I *am* mad. It's the principle of the matter.

He touches my thigh. "Grace?"

I sigh and look at him. "Yeah?"

"I really wanted to come out and pretend like everything's okay. It took me two beaches to find you. But I can't pretend we haven't fought anymore than I can ignore the fact that you hurt me. What you said about me not watching out for you enough at the Point...like that was all my fault. As if you had no role in that."

I grip the sides of my board. "It's a good thing you've got Brianna to console you." The words spew out of my mouth like a plume of smoke from a volcano about to blow. It's like I can't help myself.

He pulls away from me. "Dang straight. Heck, you even gave her the thumbs-up. So is that why you're acting like this? Somebody is interested in me and I take her out on a date. And you're jealous. All your drama. It's ridiculous. I deserve someone who appreciates me. Someone who wants me. Drama? This isn't me. I can't stand it."

I narrow my eyes. I'll give him drama. Like he hasn't been jealous of Damien all summer? I steel myself not to look into his eyes, knowing they'll melt my resolve. I've got to do what's best for me right now, and that includes protecting myself from all guys, Ford included.

"I've got news for you, Ford Watson," I say. "It's fine with me if you want to take Brittany out. In fact, Damien and I went on our own little date after the Point that day."

"Are you kidding me? Damien?" He shakes his head side to side, slowly. He seems to be realizing something I've been worried about all this time—that I'm not worth it. Then he says, "I don't know you anymore. I'm out for reals this time."

I think it's the word *anymore* that hurts the most. It feels like salt water in my eyes...and up the nose. But I take it. I deserve it. Because in the end, I know it doesn't matter.

He paddles away from me until he catches a ride in.

I sit on my board, watching him from behind. My world just went from color to black-and-white, and I'm too worn to do anything about it.

———

I walk into our house with slightly pink cheeks, hoping no one will notice and wondering what my parents are both doing home. I am so busted.

The first thing I see is the two of them sitting on the couch, lit up like neon lights, waiting for me—I freak out on the inside. I'm in big trouble, but I can't figure out what I did that was so bad they both decided to come home at the same time. Did Mom figure out I haven't started the college essays?

Mom greets me with a smile and says, "Hey, honey."

Now I'm really freaked.

I stand on the welcome mat, hoping to God I'm not dripping water and not wanting to go in any further. Did I rinse all the sand off my feet? And crap, I forgot an extra sand-free towel to use when I enter the house. Of all the days to—

"Grace, why don't you come sit down with us?" Dad points to a leather chair.

I pat at my rear end. Yep. Still wet. "Um, I know I'm wearing shorts, but I'm also wearing my swimsuit bottoms underneath them. They're still damp."

Mom says, "No big deal, sweetheart. It's just leather. Take a seat, we've got exciting news for you."

I look back and forth between them and cautiously take

a seat. On her leather chair. In my wet swimsuit. This is the Twilight Zone.

Dad says, "Tomorrow is your big day to shine, Grace."

Crazy. Aliens have inhabited my parents' bodies. Unsure, I say, "Yeah. I mean, yes sir."

Mom leans forward, excited. "Jack, tell her about it!"

What the crap? She sounds like a game show host.

Dad totally plays into her charade, booming, "You've been invited to a private, unofficial Ivy League schmooze!"

"What?" My emotions are in overdrive and the warning sensors in my brain are starting to go off. Retreat is not an option though.

Mom places a hand on Dad's forearm and leans forward eagerly. "You know Warren Driscoll, one of the senior partners at your dad's firm?"

I nod in slow motion. I've heard the name on occasion, followed by a string of curse words.

Mom continues. "Well, he's hosting the brunch, and he remembered Dad mentioning that you're hoping to go to one of the Ivies, and we got an official invite." She ends an octave higher from sheer excitement.

I'm floored. Totally blindsided. Brunch? The comp starts in the morning. But I'm not going to cry. I have to keep it together and figure out how to get out of this nightmare. Breathe in. Breathe out.

"He sent you an invitation the day before his party... isn't that kind of last minute?"

Dad snorts. "More like a last-minute email, but who the hell cares? It's an opportunity for you to impress some

Ivy Leaguers and for me to show the senior morons—I mean partners—exactly what they missed in that last advancement round."

Panic sets in. Now it's not just about the Ivies but my dad's status. After all, my success is an extension of his success. This is bad. Really bad. My chest constricts. Sweat beads up above my lip. I manage to maintain a semblance of control. "But I've been training for a surf competition all summer. It's tomorrow morning, and it's really important to me. The UCSD surf coach is going to be one of the judges. This is my chance to see where I stand."

Mom rolls her eyes. "Grace Parker, you will not ditch this once-in-a-lifetime opportunity for a silly surf competition that we've never even heard of, much less approved. We're talking about your future here. Get your head on straight."

I blink. Yeah, we're talking about my future. My chance. My once-in-a-lifetime shot to make a great impression on the UC San Diego surf coach in a competition setting. And now that's getting blown out of the water by a senior partner that Dad can't stand.

"But I've been training all summer. This comp—there's not going to be another one like it." Tears spill out. I'm breaking, fracturing into a million little pieces.

Dad leans forward, lightning fast. He's not playing game show host anymore. I lean back, his finger in my face.

"You will attend this party," he snaps. "You will be there right on time. You will not screw up this opportunity."

So this is what it comes down to—all my hard work gone because Mom wants me to go to school where it snows. And is this Dad's opportunity or mine? What's the point? The freaking point is I want to go to UCSD. I've worked hard for this.

Forget the tears. I'm furious. I stand up, trembling with anger, and take in a shaky breath. "I'm … going … to … the … comp. Just because you get thrown a last-minute bone doesn't mean I have to eat shit and smile pretty with you."

Both parents pop off the couch in disbelief that their precious robot got a spine. Dad takes two gigantic steps and stops inches from me. Inches from totally losing it in front of Mom. Everything turns slow motion for me. She joins him and places a hand on his arm, a reminder she's watching. Well, good, maybe he'll lose it. Maybe she'll see I'm not making it up. Although judging by her reaction, I have to wonder how much she really questioned my "stories" after all. It seems that as long as we pretend everything and everyone at our house is nice, then it doesn't matter what really goes on behind closed doors. If you live a lie long enough, I guess you eventually believe it.

Dad balls up his fists. "You sure as hell will go. And you *will* smile pretty and make us proud. The brunch starts at eleven a.m. Your mom and I will arrive together, as we have a parents-only mimosa mixer beforehand. You will drive the Jeep, top on, freshly washed, and wearing an appropriate dress. End of discussion."

Question: How do you win against someone who's stronger and holds the power? Answer: You don't. You just get bruised up trying.

I lock my bedroom door, crank up the music, and sneak out of my window. Even though Ford and I just had one of the worst fights ever, I know he'll understand this. How much it hurts to be told I can't compete in the comp. We've worked for this all summer.

I pedal up his driveway, second-guessing this decision and thinking maybe I should have called. What if he turns me away?

I knock on his door, heart pounding. Head throbbing.

Mama Watson answers the door. She looks confused. "Hi *mija*. Come on in."

I step inside. "Is Ford around?"

She shakes her head no, quiet. Hesitating. She sits down on the couch and pats it. "He's hanging out with Brianna."

I sink onto the couch, crying. My whole world has crumbled, and I have nobody.

Mama Watson puts an arm around me, holding me until I'm done crying it out. Even though there's nothing but a big empty hole inside me, at least I feel calmer.

I squint at her through puffy eyes. "Thanks for letting me cry."

"Sometimes that's the best thing for us."

I nod and sniffle. "Yeah."

She gets this mom look of concern on her face. "Do you want to talk about it?"

No. I don't want to talk about it with anyone but Ford. And he's not here. He's done with me. I treated him like crap. And now I don't even have a friend. I double over and bawl my eyes out again, in Mama Watson's lap. She pats my hair and I cry over more things than I can focus on—until I'm too tired to cry.

I sit up, feeling like the marshmallow man. Mama Watson passes me a box of tissues. I grab a few and wipe at my cheeks.

She says, "Would you like to talk now, *Mija*?"

I do, but I'm afraid that if I start talking everything will gush out of me like I'm a compromised dam. And fear of what will happen then—whether she believes me or not—holds me back. Even though things are messed up at home, I do love my parents, and I know they love me. I love surfing … and Ford. But he's moved on. After cinching my emotions tight, I shake my head.

She reaches out and tucks my hair back so she can see my face. "*Mija*, I know you really wanted Ford to be here. He'll be back later. You two can work things out. But I want you to know, Ford, he's just a boy. A great boy. *El te ama mucho. Pero* he can't fix whatever is this wrong. It took me a long time to learn this, but once I did, life got so much easier. The only person who can make the decision to help you is you. And the only place to put your trust is God. *¿Entiende?*"

I nod. "*Si*." Part of me wonders if Mama Watson's God is my God. I think about the reverence on her face when she makes the sign of the cross after mealtime prayers. Or how she's so positive that He's the answer. It's like I'm watching her relationship with God through a glass window. My face pressed up against it. And my God hangs out in the foyer of our church, working on more important things, while I run down the halls of my house trying to escape my dad.

I get up. "Thanks."

She stands up and hugs me. It feels good. Safe. "Anytime. I'm always here. I love you like my own, *mija*. When you're ready to talk, I'm here."

thirty

¿Que dijale?: *What does it tell you?*

It's six a.m. on a Saturday morning and I should still be in bed. But today is the surf comp. Grace will be out there without me. And then there's last night with Brianna. Blew me away. Didn't expect things to go there again. It's weird, kissing someone I'm not even exclusive with, and I don't know how I feel about it. How Brianna feels about it. Making out with her so soon. I mean, kissing her is amazing—her lips are so smooth and soft. But I'm not sure it's the right thing to do. Which sounds crazy. Everything's crashing together all at once.

I bang around the kitchen looking for cereal.

"You trying to break my cabinets?"

I whip around, embarrassed. "Sorry. Couldn't sleep."

Ma adjusts the tie on her robe and bustles into the kitchen. She waves a hand at the barstools. "Take a seat. You need my *migas* and some coffee and some sense talked into you."

I slump onto the barstool, exhausted. "Thanks."

Ma goes into cooking mode and whips everything out with the ease of a person who hasn't lost a wink of sleep. She peeks out from behind the fridge. "So, you and Grace are having problems?"

I bury my face in my arms, in a cross between exhaustion and embarrassment. Ma can read my face like a book—there's no way I want her looking at me if we're talking about Grace or Brianna. She'd kill me. "Yeah."

The refrigerator door shuts. "Grace came by yesterday."

"She did?" I sit up. "How was she?"

Ma opens the carton of eggs. "Seems like she's having a bit of a hard time."

I drop my head back in my arms. "That's just Grace. She's a drama queen."

Bam. Ma whacks my head. Not like it hurt. Just the normal *watch it* gesture.

"Okay. Okay. That wasn't nice."

The sizzle of an egg hitting the pan is the sound of love and forgiveness. Ma says, "You know, regardless of what's going on between you two, she could use a friend right now. I didn't raise you to turn your back on someone in need."

I groan. Here comes *migas* with a side of guilt.

The clang of the wooden spoon against the cast-iron skillet is fast-paced. Ma's biting back words. Which makes me feel guiltier. I already feel like a louse for dating Brianna when part of me is still attracted to someone else. Now Ma is telling me what a crummy friend I'm being to Grace. But after all the crap Grace has pulled this summer, that thought irritates me.

I sit up. "What about Grace? She hasn't been the greatest friend in the world either."

Ma shakes the spoon at me. "*Mijo*, she's not my kid. You are. Isn't today her big moment? Her competition?"

I squirm on the stool. "Yes. But I doubt she wants me there. We aren't exactly talking."

Ma turns back to the stove, dumps some chorizo in with the eggs, and stirs ferociously. "Which explains the reason she stopped by yesterday. I *always* want to share my problems with the people in my life I don't like or trust."

Guilt served. Well done. Not too sure I'll enjoy breakfast now. "But mom, what about her whole *we can't date but you can't date anyone else either* crap? And what about her going out with Damien? And she told me to date Brianna—what's that about? It's like she wants to hold me back but at the same time she doesn't want me. She's *loco*."

"How do you feel about Brianna?"

Ouch. My stomach burns. "I don't know. She's really smart, and beautiful … " I slump to the counter, realizing for the first time that I'm doing the same thing to Brianna that Grace has done to me. Well, sort of. Brianna deserves someone who is 100 percent into her. 'Cause she's awesome. And I'm an idiot who's still hung up on someone who doesn't want me. "But … "

Ma puts *migas* on two plates and sprinkles them with *cotija* cheese. She raises an eyebrow. "But what?"

I grab my plate and shove a bite of *migas* in my mouth. Then I answer, "She's not Grace."

Ma parks in the stool next to me. "Care to elaborate?"

I think about how I've made out with Brianna. That I'm not into her enough to kiss her like that. About feeling guilty, like I'm using her or something—like we're friends with benefits, but she's not in on the fact that this whole deal is a friend thing.

I shrug, ears burning. I screwed up big time, and Brianna doesn't deserve this. I owe her a major apology.

But I don't elaborate. I just say, "Not really. Besides, dating Grace isn't going to happen. I don't even think I really like her anymore. She's not into me, and she's definitely completely unavailable. So that's that." I think again about what her dad would do to my future career if I went after his daughter, and about possibly screwing things up for Hien. That's a cold shower. "Really. I don't want to date her. I just need to get over her."

Ma's eyebrows scrunch together. "Are you two still friends?"

"I don't know. It's all screwed up."

Ma says, "But she wanted to talk to you yesterday."

"She's gone on a date with Damien. I don't know if I can deal with that."

Ma points her fork at me. "Then you aren't the boy I thought you were. Are you so innocent? Can you throw the first stone, *mijo*? Grace has been a good friend to you. Remember when PoPo died? Who was there for you?"

Grace.

Ma shakes her fork at me. "You're at the age where you have to make big decisions. Keeping friends is important. Grace is important. This competition is important *to her*."

"I know, I know. But I don't know how to fix it."

She says, "Get your rear end in your truck and hit the road."

Even though I know that's what I need to do, I'm worried. The two of us didn't exactly part on good terms. "But—"

"Sometimes you rely on faith. You believe in the things you cannot see. Trust your heart. *¿Que dijale?*"

thirty-one

Eddie would go.
—Mark Foo

I barely slept last night. All I could think of was attending the comp and facing the wrath of my parents, or attending the stupid Ivy League party and schmoozing with people who might give me some incredible rec letters for colleges I don't want to attend. And oh, bonus, I'd miss out on the opportunity of my life—the surf comp I've trained for . . . with Ford, who's probably done with me . . . where one of the judges is the surf coach for UCSD.

It should be such a no-brainer, right? Go to the comp. Screw the last-minute party invite to buddy up to people I don't know or care about. But what happens if I do all that and don't advance past the first round of the comp? It would all be for nothing.

But the thing that really kept me up was the other part

of the *what happens if* question. If I skip the party, what will Dad do to me when Mom's not home? It's bad enough when I set him off randomly—forget doing something on purpose. I can't even fathom what would be waiting for me at home this afternoon. Mom's likely to give the *I'm disappointed in you* speech and the angry *how could you embarrass us by not showing up* speech, but when it's just me and Dad—which is inevitable—what will he do? Sure, I can handle being cussed out, and yeah, usually his violence is erratic and who knows what will really set it off, but this scenario is premeditated. It's an *I know I'm gonna piss you off beyond belief when you're standing there without your trophy daughter to show off* scenario.

After a night of no sleep, I still don't have any answers on how bad it would be.

The one thing I do know is that I'd regret skipping out on the comp for the rest of my life.

And that's my answer. Maybe that's kind of what Mama Watson was talking about.

While I spent the night panicking over what to do, my parents were up late yelling. That's working in my favor now, as they've slept late instead of getting up and running errands this morning. There's no way I could go through with this if I had to talk to them right now. I'd be freaking out too much. Of course, I'm counting on the note I leave on the counter to work in my favor, too:

*Good morning! I know y'all have a busy schedule
before the brunch. I'm headed out to wash the Jeep
and take care of a few things myself. See you later.*

Love, Grace

Everything's loaded and ready. I back the Jeep out of the
driveway with the lights off and hope to God they don't hear
it. I don't turn the lights on until I'm out of our neighborhood.

I hope the note buys me the time I need. I'm heading
for the comp. I'll be on the waves—where I belong—when
the brunch starts.

I speed down the highway, wishing Ford was here with
me. The image of him paddling away from me...well, it
hurts. I'm wrapped up in my own world the entire ride to
the comp. I pull into the crowded parking lot emotionally
exhausted. Lack of sleep equals shaky Grace. My body's
humming like it's filled with a thousand bees, and all I can
do is move at the speed of their wings.

The place is packed—people of all ages milling about
unloading their cars, teenage girls carrying their boards. If
that wasn't enough of a reminder that today is anything
but normal, the tents and banners are reassurance that yes,
today is the Day. That yes, I skipped out on my parents.
And all the people here, in groups or as families, make the
ache in my stomach that much bigger.

Being alone around crowds of people is way worse than
being alone by myself.

I munch my second bagel and slurp the last of my coffee. Then I take a deep breath and pray my first real prayer with all my heart.

Mama Watson's God? Everything's screwed up. I'm screwed up. I need your help. I'd really appreciate it, you know? This is weird, talking to you like this, but Mama Watson seems so sure of you. And if I could have anybody in the world on my side, well, it seems like you'd be the best option. Um, thanks.

I hold back on making the sign of the cross. Not sure about that. And while it felt a little awkward, my heart feels lighter, like it's floating in a little puddle of hope.

I sling my duffel bag over my shoulder, unload my board, and walk to the sign-in tent. There are about ten other girls in line already and I fall in behind them. It seems like several of them know each other from other surf comps. A few of them look familiar, but I feel way behind the curve. Like I should have been doing these my whole life, not entering my first one at seventeen. Everyone else seems to have some sort of cheering squad, whether it's family or friends. I've got nobody. How's that for Loserville?

Twenty minutes later, I reach the front of the line, where a cute Asian guy with blue tips on spiky bangs is checking people in.

He shoots me the pearly whites. "You got your paper-work all filled out?"

I rock back and forth on my tiptoes. "Yep."

He glances over the page and then back at me. "This your first comp?"

I pull at my board shorts. "Yep."

He grins. "You nervous?"

I'm noticing a pattern here; I give him a tiny smile. "Yep."

"Can you speak more than one word at a time?"

My tiny smile breaks wide open. "Nope."

He hands me my comp shirt. It has the number 15 on it. "Well..." He looks back at my paperwork. "Well, Grace Of One Word, I've got two for you: good luck."

I take the shirt, feeling sheepish. It kind of seemed like he was flirting with me. But my heart's taken—and broken. So much for playing it safe. There is no safe.

The girl behind me huffs, and I realize I've been standing here like an idiot holding up the line. Mr. Flirty of Two Words winks at me; I move on.

I try to ignore all the other competitors milling around, but I can't help it. Some of the girls seem nervous; others look pretty sure of themselves. Those girls are grouped together talking smack, swapping stories, and laughing. There are a few girls in the zone... they're stretching, doing yoga, and chilling out with their board watching the waves. This last group, they're my kind. I find an open spot, lay down my board, and stretch as I watch the ocean roll in— thick strands of loosely woven linen rumbling toward the shore.

Every few minutes, I stare at the number 15 printed on the bright blue T-shirt. That could be my lucky number, or a number to forget.

It doesn't matter how many times I survey the crowd, Ford hasn't shown up. I keep thinking he will, because Ford's that kind of guy. But the countdown is ticking and he's not here.

Another half hour goes by as the beach fills with spectators. All these people to watch me crash and burn, or to score the ride of my life. I'm really here. I'm really doing this. It feels surreal.

All the contestants are called into the official tent, where a hot guy with bleached-out hair, a killer tan, and dreads rehashes all the rules for us—as if we haven't lost sleep memorizing them. Because there'd be nothing worse than getting disqualified. After he wishes us luck and gives us our heat numbers, we spill out of there like a bunch of kids on a playground.

I wax my board and focus on different moves I want to try. I need to think about all the moves I can make, ones that will impress the judges. Maybe I should play it safe, pull the moves I could do in my sleep.

After all the training Ford and I did this summer, I really want him here. He's my glue; he keeps me together, and today I really need that—him. Just thinking about doing this on my own freaks me out.

I can't think about that, though. Or him. Or how much I want him or need him. It's pointless. He wanted depth. I wanted to stay in the shallow end because I was too scared to jump off the high dive without floaties.

An air-horn blares and the first heat begins. They paddle out to the breakers. I comb the wax and notice the moves girls are pulling. Some are pretty sweet. Moves I haven't tried, but they don't necessarily earn more points than the moves I've worked on—floaters, backside snaps, closeout snaps, and airs. And as Ford said during one of our workouts, "A badass move that's poorly executed doesn't impress the judges, but it does affect your score. So learn 'em and own 'em."

A few heats later, I'm up. My stomach lurches. Stepping into the water to paddle out, next to a competitor who looks like she does 360s for her warm-up, intimidates me. I hope no one can tell I'm trembly. We paddle to the waiting area, which is cordoned off by floating buoys and sponsors' signs. She's a couple of inches taller than me, and ripped. I noticed she wasn't mouthing off beforehand and she didn't act nervous. She seems calm and intense, if those traits can possibly coexist.

We sit on our boards like they're race horses, waiting for the gun. Our cue sounds and we paddle hard to be the first to catch the incoming waves. The first one rolling toward us is perfect; I stare at it, mesmerized, and wonder what Ford would say about this wave. Crap. I should be catching it, not thinking about it. The other girl gets it and I back off, waiting for the next ride. We didn't even paddle-battle.

Shit. Pull it together, Grace.

Here comes one, rolling at me full throttle. I paddle with everything I have and drop in and cut back and forth across the wave. I zip across to hit the lip, where I boost some kickass air before landing. I pull a couple of floaters and exit high on adrenaline.

My first real ride in a comp and I kicked ass! I'm higher than high right now, but I have to focus on the next wave.

We both get in a couple more rides before the air-horn blows. We immediately quit what we're doing and paddle in. Even catching a fun wave on the way in and front-porching it would earn a DQ. Nobody who's serious about competing would catch a ride in. It'd be nuts.

The morning rounds are intense, and I keep reapplying sunscreen, looking around, trying not to freak out when I see someone who has my dad's haircut. It's like being a prisoner on death row. You know there's only so much time before they're coming to get you.

I make it through quarterfinals, and then wait to find out who makes it past the semifinals. I think I caught some sweet rides my last round, but I was so focused on my waves that I have no clue how the other girl did. I'm sitting here by myself, of course. No friends here to support me. But hey, I've got free water and granola bars.

I consider checking my voicemail, but I don't even want to know how many messages are waiting for me. If I saw my parents' number on the screen right now, even once, it might be enough to send me running back, tail between my legs, and I can't do that.

The blue-haired guy walks out of the judge's tent with the sheet. The one that could mean this was all for nothing, or prove I was right to skip out on brunch with a bunch of old geezers. Four of us bombard the guy as he pins up the paper we're all dying to see.

I hang back a little waiting, to see how the other girls

respond, gauging their reactions and hoping I advanced. One girl pulls her hoodie up over her head like she's trying to hide and walks away. I hear a couple of sniffles and wonder if I'll be joining her. The girl from my last heat shrugs. And a girl who I saw making sick moves look like a cakewalk, the one I decided to call Super Girl—well, she walks away smiling.

I'm not sure what the shrug meant. It could go either way. Was the shrug an *I knew I'd make it* shrug? Or was it a *that's the way the cookie crumbles* shrug? Maybe she can shrug it off, but her shrug could mean everything to me.

I close my eyes, and then open them and shuffle over to the paper—to see my name listed as one of two girls advancing to the finals. It's all I can do not to whoop and holler and dance around and celebrate and be silly, but that's not something you do alone.

A girl with pink highlights says, "You caught some bitching rides earlier. Better watch out. Ann's not going to give you shit in finals. She's the fave."

The gravity of this moment hits me, and all happy feelings get sucked out of me. So, yeah, I made it to the finals, but what if I drop in late or wipe out? I've seen the other girls—who should have advanced but didn't. They're full-on hardcore. It's not like they gave any freebies. Whichever surfer girl walks away with the trophy and the prizes will have had a platinum heat. And I'm not sure how I'll stack up against Ann. She pulled sick moves in earlier heats and made them look like a cakewalk.

I lug my board over to the roped-off area for contestants.

We have about ten minutes to get ready. I bend down and pull a bit of wax out from the ankle of my wetsuit. My board probably doesn't need any more wax, but it couldn't hurt. It gives me something to do—an outlet for my nerves. I rub the wax over it in a hard circular motion until it's nothing but a nub.

I glance over at Ann, Super Girl. She's standing quietly, waiting for the horn to let us know we can paddle out. Nerves of steel. She glances over at me; I'm still staring at her. She flashes a smile and says, "Good luck."

My stomach flutters. I say, "Yeah, you too."

The horn blares and we both jump. I laugh awkwardly. She's all business. She swings her board in the air and races toward the water. I snap to attention and follow her, feeling foolish.

By the time I'm paddling out for the big showdown, the acid in my stomach's lurching around like ocean waves. Win or lose, the impending doom of going home has me freaked out. And then I can't let go of the fact that Ford's not here. I really am going it alone.

I make it to the waiting area a few yards behind Super Girl. We eye each other and exchange tight smiles. There goes the signal. I paddle my ass off to make it first to the incoming set. But all the worries rolling around in my mind haven't let go.

I try to ignore them and drop in first. Well, craptastic. Timing was off. I'm at the bottom when all the water's going up, which means I get sucked up the free escalator ride to the top, knowing I'm going to get pitched forward and pummeled when it crashes.

I cringe as my board and I fly over the falls and tumble down below. There goes valuable time down the tubes. The full force of the water slams me around and I curl up, trying to protect myself.

Stupid me. Holding back. Getting nailed by the damn wave. Crashing. Like in my relationship with Ford.

For a split second everything becomes clear. Life is like surfing. You hold back scared—you miss the ride. That simple.

I finally get spit out of the wave, jerk my board toward me, grab it, and paddle hard. I'm not crashing anymore, anywhere. No holding back.

I skip the next wave that comes my way. Not that I can cherry-pick, but I probably only have time for one solid ride, which means I better catch a kickass wave. The second one passes and I get antsy. It's the third one rolling my way I want. I can feel its energy.

I zero in on the sweet spot and catch it. I drop down the face. Pull my bottom turn. Carve a couple of times up and down, getting a feel for the ride, and then I go for it.

The 360. For all the times I didn't.

For me.

I attack the lip. My board goes vertical and begins the spin. I move my feet as the board and the wave do their thing. I lean back as the board almost finishes the rotation, slide my foot forward, grab the tail, and push down a little so my nose doesn't plow under. And just like that, the maneuver's over.

Awwww yeah!

I pump my fist in victory. But my ride's not over—I pump my legs to gain speed. I slip up the face of the wave, pull a floater, and boost some air before I exit. I paddle back to try to catch one more ride, but right as I begin to go for it, the air-horn blasts and I bail.

As I cruise back to shore, I wonder if that ride was enough. What does the UCSD coach think? Would a second-place finish catch his eye? I also wonder what Ford's doing, and what's going to happen when I go home.

Super Girl and I make it back to shore at about the same time. There's a bunch of guys on the beach cheering for us. We look at each other, not knowing the outcome. I look around in search of a friendly face, feeling alone and smiling so big it hurts.

My heart pumps faster—Ford's barreling at me. He doesn't slow down. As soon as he reaches me, he flings his arms around me, picks me up, and spins us until I'm dizzy and laughing.

When my feet hit the ground, I say, "You made it." Because I'm the Queen of the Obvious.

"You were awesome! I almost had to do a double take and make sure I wasn't watching someone else." He reaches out and holds my hands in his. "You didn't hold back."

Shivers run through me. "You came."

Ford stares me right in the eyes and says, "Yeah, I did." His eyes say so much more than his mouth.

Guilt—for all our stupid arguments, for holding out on him all summer, for acting dumb—hits me like a truck. It was super messed up. Like me. I swallow my fear and hope he'll give me a second chance. "I'm really sorry about everything," I whisper. "When I bunked that first wave, it was heavy. Everything hit me. And I realized how big I've screwed up."

He drops my hands and nods a few times, taking in my apology. "Dang straight. So?"

I scrunch my face. "So, what?"

"So are we friends?""

I smile. "Best." Then I can't stop myself from asking, "What about Brianna?"

His face turns red and he shrugs his shoulders. "It's not going to work out. She deserves more. I called her on the way up here." Then he hums and works his mouth like talking is a struggle. "Um. What about you and Damien? Are you two together?"

A slow smile spreads across my face. I shake my head no. He grins and steps toward me.

I spring forward on tiptoe and give him a kiss. Not a tongue-down-the-throat kind of kiss, but a soft one, a lips-melting-into-each-other-making-me-swoon kiss.

He pulls back and says, "So you don't like me, huh?"

I push at him, playfully.

He pulls me closer to him and I hug him fiercely, trying to keep it together. All my pent-up emotions from today are busting at the seams. Having Ford here with me makes me feel invincible—like I can face anything. Even home.

We pull back and hold hands and then we notice people staring. A lot of people. I'll bet money my whole face is bright red from embarrassment. Kahuna Pete walks over and says,

"I don't mean to break this clam bake up, but they've called your name on the speaker system twice now. One more go and they may decide Ann should win."

thirty-two

all in: *if a poker player goes all in,
he's betting all the chips he
has left toward the pot*

Well, shit. I fly down 101, excited about Grace's victory. She rocked it. And I'm caught up in this new Grace—the one who goes full force, no holding back. Our kiss was an emotional high. While I want to keep my head in the clouds because I'm stoked about finally kissing her, the reality of us being together is sinking in. Her dad's going to kill my career. So I can't officially date her. Not now. There's got to be some way to keep our relationship under wraps. Surely she'll understand about going for your dreams.

But in any case, we're finally together. A couple. Although I can't shout it from the rooftops. Or brag to the guys at the beach, or at poker night at Hop's. To the coffee girl at Lola's. To Teresa. Hop. And then Brianna's face hits me and a slight pang makes me sicker. She's an awesome girl. Smart. Hot. And super cool. I hate that I might have hurt her.

Nope, no sharing this good news. In fact, it doesn't even feel good, really. What was I thinking? Too much like jumping out of a plane without a parachute.

I shake it off. Try to focus on the positive. Grace winning. I'm so proud of her. She pulled a freaking 360.

Maybe Mr. Parker is all bark and no bite. Maybe he'll come to his senses about Grace surfing at UCSD and dating a local. Grace was nervous about going home since she skipped out on some brunch. But surely when her parents, especially Mr. Parker, find out she won, they'll be proud. They'll finally get that when it comes to surfing, she's all in.

I blast down 101, the sick feeling taking over. I didn't imagine it like this. I always thought I'd feel like I had the world in the palm of my hands—because finally, when it comes to me, Grace is all in.

But all I can think is *Shit, there goes my future*.

thirty-three

*I want freedom for the full
expression of my personality.*
—Mahatma Gandhi

On the drive home, three things keep running through my mind: The dream conversation I had with the UCSD surf coach, who encouraged me to go to tryouts before fall semester and said he'd make sure to let the admissions people know to look out for my application. The kiss Ford gave me on the beach. My parents' reactions.

When I arrive at the house, the driveway is empty. I wonder if my parents are driving around somewhere or if one of them is waiting for me. Throw-up hits the back of my throat, and what started as a headache on the way home is now a monster. I park the Jeep and enter through the back door by the kitchen.

And there's Dad, waiting at the table for me. He surveys

me and nods toward my spot. There's a pile of college books and mostly blank Ivy League apps in front of him. I close the door behind me and swallow hard. Then I sit.

Dad starts off. "I'm really disappointed in you, Grace. You skipped out on the brunch for a surf comp? You left a note to mislead us?"

This might be the first time he's ever been this pissed and acted rational—like a parent should. The tiniest smidgen of hope that things will work out balloons in my chest.

"Your mother and I were extremely embarrassed," he continues. "How do you think that made me look in front of my boss?" My gut curls. The vein in his neck is pulsing. "I'll tell you how it made me look. Like I have no control over my family and an ungrateful bitch for a daughter who can only think about herself and having fun. Do you really think a stupid surf comp is going to get you anywhere in life?"

His icy stare sends chills down me.

I hold my breath. It's now or never. I can be rational too. Quick breath. "Dad, I've been meaning to tell you and Mom. I really don't want to go to an Ivy League—"

"You *ungrateful* little bitch." Dad lunges at me with a solid slap.

I reel back, pressing my hand against my stinging cheek.

He raises his hand again and stops. Then he storms out of the kitchen, passing the college books on the kitchen table. He grabs the books, reels around, and charges at me.

I jump out of my chair, knocking it over, and by the time I make it to the fridge, he's within a foot.

"You want to go to college. Here's the damn books. Figure it out yourself."

He shoves the books so hard at me that even though I try to catch them they slam into my chest. It knocks the wind out of me and I slide to the floor, dropping the books at my feet. Papers scatter in all directions.

He's standing there barely reigning himself in.

The Mount Vesuvius in me erupts. I stand up, leaning against the fridge. "How dare you! How dare you!" I'm half-sobbing, half-screaming. "If you ever touch me again, I'll leave and never come back! Do you hear me! Never!"

His face registers shock, and for once he steps back. A flash of intense anger passes across his face. He clenches his fists and starts to leave the kitchen, but Mom's blocking the entrance. I'm so upset I'm shaking. She finally saw the show. Dad's going to get it. She'll finally leave him. God, that almost makes it worth it.

Mom says, "Hold up. You two aren't going anywhere. You've both said enough for one day."

Both? Both? I haven't even started.

"In fact, you've said enough for a lifetime. Grace, what were you thinking, ditching the brunch?"

My mouth drops open. I start to say something but I don't have any words.

Mom holds up her hand like she's the only saint in the room. "And Jack, you know I love you, but you get way too worked up sometimes."

Dad stands there looking uncomfortable.

Vesuvius erupts a second time. I yank down the neck of my shirt to show her red marks from where the corners of the books collided with me, small though they may be. "Look! Look what he did to me."

Mom frowns and glares at Dad. "I'll deal with that later." She looks back at me. "But that is no excuse for *your* behavior today. *You* wrote a note full of lies. You *skipped* the brunch, which is the reason your father lost his temper." Dad crosses his arms. "He was worried sick. I was worried sick. We didn't raise you to be like that. My goodness. And in the end you *embarrassed* us, in front of all the important people at his firm." Mom's eyes tear up. She glares at Dad too. "I'm ashamed of both of you." She gestures toward the table. "Now, let's all sit down and be reasonable."

I take a seat and stare at the patterns of the grains of wood in the kitchen table. Dad sits between me and Mom.

She takes a shaky breath. "So, here's the deal."

My dad slaps the part of the table I'm staring at. "Look at your mother when she's talking to you."

I sigh and look at her, doing my best to keep back tears.

"You are grounded for your behavior. You will apologize to your father and me for missing the brunch. You'll write a note of apology to his boss. We'll come up with a reasonable explanation for your absence. You and Ford are no longer to hang out and your surfboard is confiscated as of today."

I jerk upright. "What!"

Mom continues. "You will spend your senior year ensuring your class rank. If you embarrass us like this again or refuse to live in our house under our rules, then you can find another place to live. After all the years we've set aside money for you, taken you to gymnastics, taken you to Girl Scouts, taken you all over the place, I do *not* understand how you can stab us in the back. If you're going to act like that, don't come crawling to us for anything. Got it?"

I nod and keep my mouth shut.

"Now, you can go to your room and think about your apologies and your actions today. You made some very poor choices, and I'm disappointed. I thought better of you." She eyes Dad. "*Both* of you."

I get up, push my chair back into the table, and trudge down the hallway. Once I close the door to my room, I fling myself on the bed and sob in a pillow.

By two in the morning, I'm a nervous miserable wreck. My head feels like it got knocked with the "damn books." And I refuse to apologize to Dad's boss. I'm sick of lying. And all for what? To hide their freaking problems. Mom didn't even have my back—it makes me sick. I can't believe she would buy into cutting me off so coldly. I can't live like this anymore. It's crazy. I'll go crazy.

I keep thinking about choices. If I stay here, I'll have none. If I leave, I'll have choices but no family. If I stay here, I'll have a pissed-off family but no Ford. If I stay here, things will probably get worse.

I pick up my cell and call Ford.

He answers on the second ring. "Hey . . ."

I whisper, "Um, hey." This is so embarrassing. What am

I supposed to say? Yeah, right. My heart falls to the floor in one big flop.

Ford says, "What's wrong?" The tone of his voice sounds sharp, like he's on high alert.

God, this hurts so much. I don't even wipe at the tears streaming down my face. "You remember how I said things get out of control?"

"Are you okay?" His words are staccato notes.

I cover my face with my hand. "Yeah. No. Yes, I'm fine. But I'm not." It's so confusing.

"What's wrong?" His words have a terse urgency behind them.

I gulp, because I don't want pity. And no one can really get it. No one will ever fully understand living like this. "It all happened because I skipped this brunch to go to the surf comp. When I got home, it was just Dad. Which should have been clue number one to shut up. But I didn't. And he slapped me, and hit me with books. Well, sort of. I mean he did, but it was after we argued. And my mom wants me to apologize. And I'm not explaining this very well. My head hurts and I'm exhausted and . . ." My voice ends in a croaky whisper. "I can't . . . live like this . . . anymore."

"I'll be right there. Your stuff packed?"

I hadn't even thought about the logistics. "No."

He says, "Throw whatever you can't live without in your suitcase and we'll figure the rest out later. Don't worry and stay off their radar. Okay?"

"Okay."

Silence.

Then he says, "And Grace?"

"Yeah?"

"I love you."

And that's when I break down. Between gut-wrenching sniffles, I say, "I...love...you too."

Packing my suitcase at three in the morning, figuring out necessities versus accessories, as noiselessly as possible, is like expecting a train wreck to be orderly. It's not.

I survey my room, trying to decide where to start. How do I know what I can and can't live without? I swipe at my tears with my sleeve. At this point, snot on my shirt is the least of my concerns. After a shaky breath, I shuffle over to my closet and dig out the one suitcase I own.

The reality of this nightmare feels removed from me, and instead of breaking down and bawling, I walk over to my dresser and open a drawer in search of my favorite T-shirts and board shorts. At this moment, it's too much to register. So I pretend like I'm just going on a long trip.

The first stacks of T-shirts are mostly Goodwill buys of old-school surf shirts and brands. They're worn and comfy and I don't feel bad about taking them because my mom can't stand them. But it also makes part of me ache so deep I don't know how it can ever heal. Those T-shirts aren't just surf shirts. They're memories of fun, no-strings-attached-or-apologies-needed shopping trips with Dad. He'd be in a good mood and take me to Goodwill. We'd eye the store as a challenge. How many cool, retro shirts or cords could we score that trip? Every find was like striking gold. Dad and I would leave with the biggest grins on our faces.

I can't believe I'm doing this. It's a moment I've dreamed about for years, only there's no feeling of victory. No happy dance will be carried out. I smash down my suitcase, sit on top of it, and force the zipper to slide to the other side. I set it down next to my ragged teddy bear.

Then I tiptoe down the hall in a drunken fashion, lugging my suitcase without dropping it. I go back for my backpack and then make one last sweep of my room, my old bear tucked under my arm.

As I step into the hall, I see Mom silhouetted in a doorframe. My heart leaps to my throat and a confusing shame consumes me. Mom pads down the hall toward me, putting two and two together.

She says softly, "So this is how it's going to be. You've made your choice. Just don't come back expecting anything from us. Consider yourself on your own." Her voice breaks and I see the hurt in her eyes. "You might think I'm weak for staying, but I'm a lot tougher than you could imagine. I've been through a lot more with your father than you could ever understand. Sometimes you look at me and I feel your judgment, but things aren't cut-and-dry in families, and they aren't cut-and-dry in marriages. Your father does the best he can. His neighborhood wasn't the kind you've grown up in. Your father has done more for you than *anyone* took the time to do for him growing up."

A tear trickles out of the corner of her eye. She pauses,

clenches her jaw, and pulls herself together. "Where are you planning on going?"

I swallow the lump building in my throat. "Ford's."

She narrows her eyes. "You think his parents are going to want an extra kid to be responsible for?"

I think about my polka dot mug. About the hugs, the jokes, the smiles. Ford's house is the only place I feel one hundred percent accepted. "Yeah, I do."

Mom flinches, blinks, and then stiffens. There's more reaction in that response than I can figure out. As long as I can remember, she's been an expert at not letting her guard down, at keeping up the pretense. I wonder what she thinks about the possibility of someone wanting me, no strings attached.

"I hope things work out with your new family," she says, "because otherwise, things are going to get lonely pretty quick. In this life, family is all you have."

I nod and walk resolutely toward the front door with leaden feet, Mom taking staccato steps by my side. Right before I reach it, her arm falls across the opening like she's Checkpoint Charlie. "And I'll need your house key."

The finality of her statement hovers in the air like a thick fog. I swallow, dig the key out of my pocket, and hand it over, feeling like a common criminal. My insides feel shaky and my heart just broke into a thousand new fragments. Good God, I wish she knew how much this hurts, how much I wish things were different.

She takes it and walks back down the hall like the fragile, broken woman she's become.

I go in the opposite direction. I guess, really, the one I've been headed in my whole life. Freedom.

thirty-four

situational irony: *an occasion in which the outcome is significantly different from what was expected or considered appropriate*
—www.grammar.about.com

Grace hurt. By Mr. Parker. That's what runs through my head as I knock on my parents' door at three in the morning.

My folks sleep heavy. I could throw a party and they wouldn't wake up. I pound on their door again.

Grace on the phone, crying. She's tried to tell me. She's hinted.

The lock on their door unclicks and Ma opens it, her hair in all directions. She groans, "*Mijo*, it's three in the morning. This better be good."

"Grace can't live there, Ma. Her dad hit her."

Ma snaps her eyes wide open and lets out a stream of curse words in Spanish. She's awake now. "Slow down, *mijo*. Where is Grace?"

I bounce on my toes. "She's at her place. Packing. I told her we'd pick her up. That she can move in with us." Then I wait for the bomb.

Ma nods. "Of course. Let me get dressed. I'm going with you. Put on some jeans and a T-shirt. Grab my keys."

I nod, upset and scared. For Grace. Feeling impotent. Wishing I were there already.

Ma looks at me like she gets it. She pats my cheek. "*Mijo*, she'll be fine. You're a good son. Let's get moving."

Five minutes later, Ma and I are out the door. The ride to the Parkers' is quiet. A thousand little things start flashing through my head. Clues I missed. Grace never having me over. Her parents being so uptight. Controlling. The day Grace got sliced by that kook. The lifeguard's dirty look. The bruise on Grace's hip. Things I didn't connect. Or maybe, didn't want to see. I was so focused on my freaking internship. On that letter of recommendation. On helping more Jorges. On Little Hien. I didn't see the person standing in my own backyard. A little white girl on a surfboard. My best friend.

My stomach retches. I roll down the window and stick my face out, letting salty wind blow in my face. Taking deep breaths. Trying not to throw up. Trying to reconcile how a dad can love his daughter but can't control himself. I've seen the look of pride on his face when Grace catches a good ride. I've had burgers with them at In and Out after a surf session and laughed at the same stupid jokes. It blows my mind. Mr. Parker is known for keeping his cool in litigation—it's like an incompatible computer system. My head spins with pictures of books flying at Grace.

With Mr. Parker's face laughing at something funny. Grace always sitting on her front porch 'cause she couldn't wait to get the hell out of there.

Guilt. I'm knee-deep in the shit. Trying to keep Grace from dating people to stay on her dad's good side. Not wanting to date her 'cause her old man would ruin my future. That should have set off warning sirens. Instead, I was trying to figure out how to save my sorry ass. But Grace? She's the one who needs saving.

Thinking of the stupid things that have always bothered me about my own parents makes me feel small. Like wishing Ma was more of a neat freak. Or that Dad didn't have grease worn into the skin around his nails all the time. Appearances. Who the hell cares? Reality is what counts.

Ma pulls up to Grace's house. Grace is sitting on a suitcase in the middle of the driveway, hunched over, hands tucked inside her hoodie. Ma parks, and I rush out of the car. But somehow Ma beats me to Grace. She swishes over there and sweeps Grace up in a big hug. I feel stiff and stupid. Not sure of what to do.

Grace slumps into Ma's arms. Ma strokes her hair and murmurs comforting phrases in Spanish. Then a long, dry, shuddering sob comes out of Grace. I run over and put my arms around them from the other side. It's a Watson sandwich, with Grace in the middle.

She draws strength from it and straightens up. We both pull away from her, giving her some space. I give her hand a little squeeze but don't let go. Then I bend over and get her suitcase. Ma grabs her backpack and hands Grace an old teddy bear.

The front door flings open and Mr. Parker storms out in a T-shirt and pajama pants. Shit. I wish my dad were here.

He barrels over to us. I fling my arms out in front of Grace and Ma, nudging them back. Then I step forward, between them and Mr. Parker.

He narrows his eyes. "This isn't your business." Then he glares at Grace. "You're going to leave? Think you can do better?" He spreads his arms out wide and laughs a mocking laugh. "Shoot for the moon with your dreams. Go to the local college and become a surf bum. Wow. What's the point in being valedictorian?"

I turn back to see tears running down Grace's face. Ma is too busy hugging Grace and alternating between praying and cursing in Spanish. I stare down Mr. Parker. "That's enough, Jack."

He moves forward. "Yeah, and what are you going to do about it? Really? Is she worth your future?"

I step up. "Yeah, she is. And you know what, Jack? I quit. And my future? You don't own a minute of it."

"You punkass kid." He lunges at me with a right hook.

I step left, circle my arm around his incoming fist, deflect it, grab his wrist, and twist it behind his back, yanking it upward hard enough to make him calm down. Adrenaline pumps through my body, surging to the point I'm almost shaky.

"Real men don't punch kids. Period." I twist his arm up a little tighter, so angry; it's taking all my control not to hit him. I've got to show Grace I'm different. I lower my voice and say, "Screw you and your connections."

Then I shove him to the ground, away from me. My guess is he'll be nursing his arm instead of picking a fight.

He half sobs, half yells, "I'm finished with all of you. You hear that, Grace?"

This is not the time to linger. I rush toward Ma and Grace and corral them to the car. We hurry into the SUV like that, holding hands. With broken hearts.

thirty-five

If it were not for hope
the heart would break.
—John Ray

Mama Watson turns the key in the ignition and speeds away. Then she says, "Buckle up, *mijos*."

We do, and Ford sticks to me like glue. He rests his hand on my leg, just above my knee, giving gentles squeezes every now and then.

We ride in awkward silence, absorbing the gravity of the situation. Ford told off my dad. Blocked his punch. Kept his cool. For me. There's no going back after that exit. I pick at the hem of my shorts with my free hand and when Ford notices this, I switch to tucking and untucking my hand in my sleeve. The familiar rhythm comforts me and absorbs some stress. He doesn't look down again. I stare at the floorboard, afraid to break down. Afraid I'll never be able to be put back together again.

Mama Watson turns into their neighborhood. I realize I haven't even said thank you. But no words come to the surface. My throat's as dry as a bag of cotton balls. She stops at a stop sign. I wonder how I'm going to explain things and think how much I owe them, how the warmth of Ford's hand holding mine means the world. She parks in front of their garage. The familiar grate of their gravel drive calms me.

We get out of the truck. Ford grabs my suitcase, and I carry my backpack and teddy bear. Mrs. Watson unlocks the front door and as I shove my hand in my pocket, I remember it's now void of a house key. Realization hits me: I have nowhere to call home. Loneliness sweeps through me, adding to the ache in my chest and throat. And shame. I'm so ashamed. My *everything is good* facade has been blown to a million little pieces. Now I don't even have pretend dignity.

Mr. Watson stands guard in the living room. He surveys us. "Did things go okay?"

Mrs. Watson gives him a hug. "We'll talk more about this later."

He nods. Then he hesitates and walks over. "Grace, I want you to know that you're welcome in our home." He tries to ignore the handprint on my cheek, but his eyes keep focusing on that side of my face. He wipes at the corner of his eye and escapes down the hall.

Mrs. Watson leads us into the guest bedroom and flips on a lamp. "Grace, why don't you sit in this chair? It's cushy and comfy. Ford and I will sit on the bed for a quick minute. I'm sure you're exhausted."

I sit and note the worn look in her eyes and the lack of life in Ford's.

"For tonight, we'll put you up here, in the guest room. Usually we attend mass on Sunday mornings, but we'll go tomorrow evening instead; I think we could all benefit from sleeping in as late as possible. Tomorrow afternoon, we'll regroup and sort things out—figure out how to make you feel more at home. Don't feel bad, *mija*. This isn't your fault. We'll stick by you."

Unsure of how to respond to everything thrown at me, I nod and hold back tears.

Mrs. Watson stands up. "I'm sure the best thing right now for you is sleep. And a hug. Everyone needs hugs."

She leans down and gives me a big hug that's warm and enveloping. Even when I let go, Mama Watson holds it for a second longer. Something in me melts a little. She turns to Ford. "I know you need to talk. You two have ten minutes, and then, Ford, you skedaddle to your own room. Okay?"

Ford says, "Okay."

She leaves us to bumble through our confusion. I stay seated, unable to sort out my feelings.

Ford sits facing me, his knees touching mine. He takes my hands in his.

"I'm really sorry I didn't figure things out and help you sooner. I look back at little clues I never caught, and I feel stupid. I know you think you're tough and you can take it, but *I'm* not that tough. Your bruises—little or big—they exist. That kills me."

His voice breaks, and so does another little piece of my heart. I bite my upper lip.

"You deserve so much more. Hell, everyone deserves better than this." Ford tucks my hair behind my ear and whispers, "You're safe here."

Safe.

I break down sobbing. Everything I've held in gushes out uncontrollably, and with it the noises I always suppress. And even though I'm bawling—shoulders shaking, snot flowing, full-fledged bawling—I'm crying out so many unspoken hurts. It's cleansing.

He pulls me to him and I hang on to him like he's a life preserver. Our faces touch and I realize Ford's crying too. I wonder why I didn't tell him sooner, why it took me so long to stand up for myself. And if things will ever be okay, really okay? When Ford stood up to my dad, I was in shock, but it's like he turned on a pilot light inside me, one that says I'm worth it—that I have value—that we all have value. And that is what I'm going to cling to.

Emily Dickinson once compared hope to a "thing with feathers," but I disagree. Hope is a wide-open ocean full of endless possibilities.

epilogue

The Master is his own path.
—Tuan-mu Tz'u

While waiting for my cue to walk up to the podium and speak at our graduation ceremony, I turn and scan the audience that fills the stands behind me. There's Mama Watson and Eli, huge grins on their faces, on the left side of the stadium. Mama Watson is leaning forward slightly, like a school girl eagerly anticipating her own name being called. Eli's holding his fancy Nikon camera. Turns out he's an incredible photographer.

It's funny remembering my adjustment to living with the Watsons. It was a bit clumsy, and I floundered trying to understand the dynamics of the household. It took several months for Eli to totally win my trust and for Ford and me to build a healthy relationship—one that doesn't consist of me depending on him to always come to my rescue or be there for me. The ability to stand up for one's self is just as important as the ability to stand up for others.

I turn back around and pretend like I'm listening to the five zillionth speaker, resting my hands carefully on the diploma in my lap. It's hard to believe how many things brought me to this moment in time. I know that moving out of my parents' house was the right decision, and I don't regret it. I do wish things were different with my parents, especially my mom. Her embarrassment over the situation causes her anxiety and hurt, but she has choices too.

Ford's parents both agreed I needed to talk to someone—a professional. It frustrated me incredibly at first, but having someone who's used to sorting things out has been instrumental in helping me muddle through my baggage.

The thing I find most ironic at the moment is my class rank. For the past four years, as I studied and fought to be first in my class, I considered it my ticket out of here, but my ticket out was simply my ability to walk through the front door. I'll be staying at the Watsons next year, too, and attending the University of California at San Diego.

The funniest thing that's happened has been getting accustomed to going to mass with the Watsons. For the first month, I constantly sat down, stood up, or knelt after everyone else did, and I mean *everyone*. But now I've come to enjoy the traditions and the meanings attached. I'm not sure how I feel about religion, but I do feel like I understand faith on a more personal level. It's kind of like the 360—in that crucial moment, it's all about letting go instead of holding on.

Faith seems like it's about relationship. The closer I get

to Ford and Mama Watson—see how Mama stirs the sugar into her coffee and then licks her spoon before putting it in the sink, or how Ford reads his dad's mind and passes him the wrench before he asks for it—the more I understand them, and love them. So I think God may be the same way. When I sit on the Watson's back porch and eat my *migas* with my legs tucked up under me, I watch the clouds move and wonder who made them. Who made the ocean, and those waves I love? And sometimes God and I talk. It's mostly one-sided—I talk and he listens. But sometimes, I think I might hear him back. It isn't a roar, like my dad. It's a whisper. I believe with all my heart that if I seek truth, I will find it, and that's what I plan on doing. It's what I did when I gave my mother my key. I had to know the truth about what life is supposed to be. I'm finding it with the Watsons.

I snap to when I hear Principal Ledbetter's voice reverberate through the stadium. "Let's all give a warm welcome to this year's valedictorian—Grace Parker."

I rise and make my way to the podium. Before speaking, I take a deep breath and scan the audience. I see the Watson family cheering. I scan the center of the crowd and stop at the far right corner; my heart aches. My parents are there, clapping for me. I tear up, swallow hard, and take a deep breath.

Ford pops up in his row and hollers. A teacher promptly heads over there and yanks him back down to his seat, which is of course the comic relief I need.

"Good afternoon," I say. I pull back a little, listening to my voice reverberating across the football field. *Just breathe.* I scoot in toward the microphone and look at my fellow classmates. "Valedictorians are supposed to give memorable speeches about going out into the world and becoming something. Today my speech is not about what you become, but who you are along the way."

I pause and breathe in deeply. "This past year, I've been riding waves in an ocean riddled with riptides, undertows, and awesome rides. I've learned that I'm stronger than I thought, that sometimes power comes in the ability to say no, and that life is as full as we make it." I throw my hands open wide toward the audience. "We've got our whole lives in front of us; let's remember it's as much about the journey as it is the destination.

"Confucius said, 'Our greatest glory is not in never falling, but in rising every time we fall.' We all have choices … sometimes we have to make hard ones; sometimes we're forced to make split-second decisions and then paddle for dear life. When I'm on my board and feel the swell and look over my shoulder at an epic wave, I hope I choose to ride it." I lean toward the podium and make eye contact with several students as I grip the sides of the podium. "That's what I hope for you—epic rides.

"I'd like to leave you with the words of a man whose actions revolutionized a country through a spirit of peace. Mahatma Gandhi said, 'My life is my message.' What's your message, and are you living it?"

Applause splatters across the auditorium and hats fly in the air. I hurry from the podium, anxious to join the celebration.

Besides, Ford and I have waves to catch.

Acknowledgments

So many people have read different versions of this manuscript that there is not enough space to include everyone. First, let me say thank you to Austin SCBWI for all you have done to build me up as a writer, for your encouragement, and for the wonderful fellowship you provide writers.

My sincerest thank you goes to all writer-folks who read the early versions. A special thank you to Sam Bond and Raynbow Gignilliat, who should receive medals for all the drafts of this book they read. You two are special to me in magical ways.

Thank you to Lyn Seippel, Alison Rice, Eileen Clark, Holly Green, Shelli Cornelison, Amy Rose Capetta, and Sara Kocek for critiques and encouragement.

Thank you to Nikki Loftin for all of the above, and for walking this publishing road with me. Your friendship and generosity bless me.

Thank you to April Lurie and Jennifer Ziegler for your invaluable insights in helping me push this book to the next level.

Thank you to Cynthia Leitich Smith for wisdom and encouragement. You have been a blessing.

Thank you to Meredith Davis, a kindred spirit, for your fabulous encouragement and critiques. You are a woman of graciousness.

Thank you to my first teen readers, Erin Hostetler and Brittany David, for believing in this story.

A big thanks to my extremely talented teen photographer,

Merissa De Falcis of De Falcis Photography, for taking my headshots.

Thank you to my fabulous agent, Mandy Hubbard, who believed in this book and in my writing. You are a lovely, funny, and tenacious person. I appreciate your guidance.

Thank you to Brian Farrey-Latz, my quick-witted and thoughtful editor, who believed in this book and helped me make it stronger. Thank you to the entire Flux team and to Lisa Novak for a gorgeous cover; to Mallory Hayes, publicist extraordinaire; and to Sandy Sullivan, my wonderfully detail-oriented production editor.

Thank you to my parents for instilling in me a love of literature, for encouraging my endeavors, and for buying me an incomprehensible number of books.

Thank you to my amazing husband, who has loved me well, supported my writing journey since its inception, and always cheers me on. I'm so appreciative of all you do for our family.

About the Author

Lindsey Scheibe loves writing, surfing, rock climbing, traveling, and outdoor adventures. She's been surfing since eighth grade, from Texas to Maui to Mexico, and has won competitions in rock climbing. She met her husband in a climbing gym, and now lives in Texas with her family. *Riptide* is her debut novel. Visit her online at LindseyScheibe.com.